Odyssey
Down Under
Parts IV and V

JAMES GARDNER

NEWMAN SPRINGS PUBLISHING
320 Broad Street
Red Bank, NJ 07701

First originally published by Newman Springs Publishing 2023

ISBN 979-8-88763-251-3 (Paperback)
ISBN 979-8-88763-252-0 (Digital)

Printed in the United States of America

Acknowledgments

A big thank you goes to Hannah Singhurse, who typed the manuscript for this book and also books I, II, III, and IV. Without her help on all my books, six to date, I feel they would not have ever reached completion. Her work is always quality workmanship, and it never ceases to amaze me!

And for the help of Candance Johnson, Heber Springs Print Shop. Candy worked with me on all my books to produce a quality front cover with my artwork and her trusty camera. Thank you, Candy, for all the professional help, ideas, many copies of work in progress, and professional workmanship.

And to my departed wife, Anita, I say, "Thank you for your writings, poems, awards, and three published books you left behind." Good to build memories on. You were the professional writer, but you always encouraged me. "Write a story, Jim!" So for you, James did!

Books by James Gardner

In the Quest for Quanah
Return of the White Wolf
Odyssey Down Under (First Edition)
Odyssey Down Under II (Cruise of South Pacific Islands)
Odyssey Down Under III (Cruise to Norfolk Island, New Zealand, Tasmania)
Odyssey Down Under IV (Cruise North, Singapore, Japan, Aleutian Islands, Part of Alaska, Hawaii Islands)
Odyssey Down Under IV (Return to Fiji)

Short Stories

"Suzann and James"
"One Snowy Night"
"The Cobbler"
"Sea Accident"

Odyssey
Down Under

Part IV

North to the Aleutians

Chapter 1

It was Sunday afternoon again, and one of those days you didn't know to take a nap or sit and think. The first time I took up with Captain Mobley, it was a Sunday afternoon, and I was on a comeback trip to St. Joe Island, Canada. Of all the crazy places to me, an Aussie captain sailing three-master, it was there. It was a scaled-down replica of the HMS *Vanguard*, which was always my favorite of all the old sailing ship adventures. Never believed it started there along with a caring friendship that most people would love to have.

But that journey did not end there. It came up again and again! It became like a call of the wild. Every time I heard a sail flap, I was ready to head out!

Well, here we are. Another Sunday afternoon, and I couldn't think to nap! I was too restless. I hadn't heard from Captain Mobley for a long time, and he always rattled my cage during a Sunday nap! I just need to give him a call before he calls me this time. After all, it is his Monday early morning, according to the time difference. I never could get used to that! Go there, and you lose a day. Come back, and you are back in the same day! It's all a sixteen-hour flight, no matter how you cut it!

So I rattled his phone. He answered on the second ring! "Hello, mate! How's it going down under?"

I hear that roaring laughter, and he replied, "I never thought I'd get a call from that bloke in the States." He chuckled. "And I don't mean that in a bad way, mate!"

"I figured it was getting high time you called, so I jumped the gun!"

"As a matter of fact, I was. The crew kept saying, 'Call James! Call James!' I don't know why they get so excited when something's about to come down! They like you, I guess!"

"Well, I don't know why either, Captain. I don't do much for them!"

"Yes, but they know you are always there for them, and that's what counts!"

"Thanks for that, Captain. Okay, so what's up?"

"Well, I was about to call you when I got things ironed out! It's time for us to take another cruise!"

"Oh? And where to this time, pray tell?"

"Well," he chuckled. "We are going up to see the Aleutian Islands!" He chuckled again! I just went silent! For a long time! After a while, he asked, "James, you still there?"

"Yes, I am, but are you?"

Captain roared with laughter. "Serious," he said.

"Well, you must have a lot of time on your hands for a trip like that!"

"No, James, we went all the way up to Newfoundland before we met you!"

"Okay, I guess you're right at that! What's the plan?"

"Well, James, we have to get you on board first! You up at San Diego Naval Base?"

"No, Captain. That's why I want to come to Sydney like always. It wouldn't feel right if I didn't!"

"I guess that's a yes? James?"

"It is a yes, Captain. I'll start plans." So after plans, I find myself on another flight to down under! "On the road again," so Willie sings, but I wasn't singing—I was wondering what I was getting into this time! But "nothing ventured, nothing gained" was the old jargon when I was coming up in life.

I've been on the flight enough to know that it's sixteen hours from LA to Sydney without any mishaps or diversions, and Qantas Air gives you a comfortable service and looks after your every need. As always for this long a flight, I don't go coach but pay the extra for first class—two seats! Ever since my flight to Fiji with the Fiji citizen traveling from Canada, I want to avoid some stranger sleeping on my shoulder for the duration of the night flight. Anita always got a giggle out of that one!

Plans, as usual, were to make Sydney, go directly to Menzies Hotel for rest, and shake jet lag! Then the following morning, a good morning breakfast before I walked the six blocks down to Captain Cook's docks. At every corner, there is a stoplight, and when it goes from red to green, it sounds like a pigeon clucking! This never ceases to amaze me.

Arriving at the dock where the *Sheila II* is docked, I will muster in with Captain Mobley. He will have a game plan for this cruise—or should I say, "A course charted!"

He always seems to slip in a little surprise trip, even though he has already told me where the destination will be, but knowing where on the go or the return remains to be seen!

Chapter 2

In the morning, I made my way to the dock area between clucks! And everything in the dock area looked like it was still the same as when I left last time. The vendors, the Aboriginal folks with their crafts. Next to the last ship berth, the *Sheila* lay still, but that wouldn't be for long. I imagine that within a day, Captain Mobley will be wanting to get underway for the next journey. The last berth was empty. The last time I was here, the *Endeavor* (Captain Cook's ship replica) was docked. A friend of mine had signed on her for a ten-day working cruise, and they were expected to perform just like the crew for the duration of the cruise. That must have been an exciting journcy!

Captain Mobley took me over for a tour, and it was quite a ship in its time. The original, that is hard to believe. That crew was at sea for years without ever getting back to England. So as I approached the *Sheila II*, all eyes were upon me! As I approached the gangway, the crew let out a hearty cheer. These guys sure know how to bolster a man's ego! I advanced to the top of the gangway, turned and saluted the flag aft, turned to Captain Mobley and requested, with a salute to him, "Permission to come aboard, sir?"

"Permission granted, Petty Officer James." And I boarded amid handshakes and slaps on the back! It was protocol in our navy and Captain's navy to perform this courtesy whenever you were to board or disembark your ship or any other ship.

After all the hoopla calmed down, including Cookie standing at the galley door, banging his pan, Captain Mobley chuckled and said, "Welcome home, James. Stow your gear. Today is a rest day before we get underway in the morning. We will go over the charts and destination.

"That will get you up-to-date, and I'm hoping that again, you will keep a log and some commentary on each port we visit. The crew and I love those logs, and it gives us factual events to look back on and reminisce."

"No problem, Captain. Because they serve me as well, and there are friends back home who like the read!"

Chapter 3

The next day was rest day, and I was glad! Captain wanted to give me an update on the destination, which I was anxious to hear. Captain opened the maps, and we started to look! Having no idea what was in the plan, I anticipated more South Pacific tours. When he pointed out the Aleutian Islands, I almost passed out! He chuckled at the response! I was speechless.

"No big deal, James. We have gone farther. Remember when we picked you up on the first cruise? We had been clear up the Atlantic to Nova Scotia. So distance-wise?"

"Well, Captain, it was a bit of a momentary shock! I should know by now that the world is a challenge to you. I do consider your limitations for sake of the crew! Too long out is not a good thing."

He could only smile, for he wasn't sure where I was coming from.

"What's the first stop?"

"Well, I was planning on going north through the Marianas and heading for Japan, but I changed the plans a little! We will go around the top of Australia and head into the South China Sea. Our destination is to cross the waters of Indonesia and head for Thailand. Singapore is just at the bottom of Thailand, a sparkling gem of the Orient!"

"Is this the trip surprise, Captain?"

"Well, yes. You know, I know, and Helmsman knows because it makes good sense in case we need a backup!"

"I agree, but the crew doesn't know?"

"Right, but it's really a surprise trip for all hands. Do you know about Singapore, James?"

"I know that it is the industrial and technological capital of the world. All major companies from all over the world are based there. They have the knowledge and expertise to do anything you want done—manufacturing to electronics to investments—you name it!"

"Like I said, the gem of the Orient!"

"What is our purpose?"

"I want to treat you and crew to a tour of the island and also take everyone to the new botanical gardens that were just completed."

"I can't say anymore because you have already been there?"

"I was! I took Sheila down—or should I say up—for a tour."

"You mean you actually took Sheila on your ship to Singapore?"

He laughed. "No, we flew!"

"By what airline?"

"Courtesy of Curt! I contacted him at American Samoa. He flew to Sydney, picked us up, off to Singapore for a tour, and then he flew us back to Sydney."

"Wow!" was all I could say.

"You ought to see his de Havilland seaplane now! All refurbished, new paint job, new plush seats. He can carry up to twenty people, but he prefers to cut back to fifteen or sixteen. I included him on the tour, the three of us taking in sights. I want to treat you and the crew this time!"

"That's mighty big of you, Captain. I will write a few lines about it!"

"So that's the first big blast! Then it is back out to the China Sea to the South Pacific, then heading north to Japan. I've an old friend located in Osaka. You will get details as we go. Then strike out for the Aleutians, which I have never seen, across to Alaska. Then down to the Hawaiian Islands, then back to maybe Fiji, and on into homeport. There will be stories and facts to write about, so James, sharpen your pencils and your mind."

Then Captain threw back his head and gave me one of his hearty laughs. "We will get underway in the morning. Remember, don't reveal to the crew where we are going! If they get suspicious, I'll tell them not to worry—just a little side trip!"

"Just one more question, Captain. The Aleutians and Alaska can be pretty cold at times?"

"Don't worry, James. I checked. We are going into fall and winter here, and they are going into spring and summer there. Alaska is not as severe as people think. Tough winters, yes, but on north tow and the pole is where the ice hangs in!"

"Okay!"

"Now off to your bunk, James. Sleep tight. Early call in the morning!"

"Goodnight, Cap."

Chapter 4

After a hearty breakfast and that second cup of coffee, we were ready to go! The crew was full of anxious energy anyhow about the trip to come! The gangway was pulled in, the two flags, the Aussie and US, were raised and saluted, and everybody jumped in on their duties for leaving port! Captain was ready to take the wheel when Helmsman stepped up.

"Captain, if you don't mind, I'd like to take her out! I'll take first watch for as long as you like?"

Captain smiled. "Yes, Helmsman, that would be nice. It's been a long time since I took out of this harbor with no responsibility."

So once again, I also had the privilege to get underway, leaving Sydney Harbour on the *Sheila II*. We were underway by gosh! Beautiful sunny day, a calm sea, and wind to our back! Who could ask for more? Helm at the wheel gave Captain and I leisure time to talk about what was ahead.

As we went north in the Pacific and then started to veer northeast in the Coral Sea, the crew started looking at us in question! They knew we were to go up through the Marianas and on north, but to them, we were veering off course. Captain chuckled. He knew his plan was starting to take shape!

"Don't worry, boys. Just a little change in plans. We'll take a sightseeing cruise past New Guinea and Indonesia! Maybe a shortcut?" Then he laughed. That settled the crew. They knew Captain Mobley was still in control, and they knew that, sometimes, he was full of surprises. They relaxed and went on.

(From here on, I won't talk about nights, days, distance, or who took watch because we have enough to cover on this trip without going into details. But I will say that, yes, I took my turn at watch, and at times, in a safe area, took over the wheel!)

So skirting New Guinea and Indonesia, we moved out of the Coral Sea into the Arafura Sea. It was a little touch and go through the many islands between here and the Philippines. I was glad that Captain now had the wheel!

When we broke out of this island area into the Philippine Sea, we were moving up the coastline of the islands. Captain looked at me. "James, you ever seen the Philippine islands or know anyone from here?"

"No, never been, but I knew a fellow from here. His name was Fuji."

"Well then, maybe on a future cruise we can come back through here and take in some of these islands!"

"Good enough," I remarked.

As we went up the coastline, we were due east of the Northern Mariana Islands. The crew threw up a loud cheer! They figured we had made the shortcut and were heading north, back to the Pacific. Captain held the wheel and was chuckling to himself. Later on, we veered to the east again, and the crew was looking up in confusion.

Captain said, "Not to worry, boys. Just a little side trip I want to show you!" Captain knows best, so they settled down again and began to take in the sights. Going past Malaysia, into the South China Sea, we came to the Korean straits. Passing through, heading north again, we came to Indonesia and Thailand. Off the bottom of Thailand lay the large island of Singapore!

Captain yelled, "Here we are, mates! We are going to take leave of Singapore!" A mighty cheer went up!

Singapore from the sea was spectacular! It was like approaching the Big Island of Hawaii from the sea. All the high-rise, new, beautiful buildings in the natural setting of the tropics, seeing the hustle and bustle of the city. Yes, it was a spectacular sight.

"Ever been here, James?"

"No, but I know that they cater to the world in advanced technology—electronics, manufacturing, research, business, you name it! You will see signs of all companies throughout the world. All have a base here. All have Singapore included in their various occupations. The company I worked for had a base here. They also contacted Singapore for electronic devices that would go in their end products."

"Yes, it truly is the gem of the Orient is what I say!" said Captain.

After we got docked and secured, we were called to meet! "Here's the plan of the day, mates. For the remainder, you can rest, take shore, leave, or whatever. Everyone back on board tonight. Now tomorrow is going to be a long, very long day. It will be your surprise of this voyage! At the end of tomorrow, we will decide to get underway that night or wait for daybreak."

Chapter 5

So everyone was off to bed to get some rest for a big day. As I climbed into my bunk, I told myself to rise early or be the victim of Cookie's pan! Cookie was an early riser. If everyone was not up, he would come out of the galley with his pan and ladle and bang you into reality! He was no respecter of men, either. It applied to one and all.

Laying there awake brought back a memory of when I was in the navy. We had an old salt who was in charge of getting us up in the morning. He would sneak into our compartment at exactly 5:00 a.m., put his nightstick into the metal trash can, and harshly bang it around! Brother, you were up immediately and moving on! You might not be in your right senses, but you were on the move!

Then my thoughts wandered back to the time I met Captain Mobley. It was on St. Joe Island, Canada, when he and his crew ventured up the St. Lawrence waterway into the Great Lakes for a see. They had just come down from Novia Scotia on a journey north. I was also on a journey north to Canada to relive my dreams and memories. When I caught sight of the *Sheila* docked at St. Joe, I was captivated! Then Captain Mobley approached, knew my name from the dock keeper, and things went from there. He saw that I was having a little problem with grief and invited me to sail away down under with him. That I had to give my grief a rest and build some new dreams to reflect upon.

He took me aboard for a tour, introduced me to his crew. Two retired marines, Ned and Jake, four retired sailors, Matt, Mark, Paul, and Barnabas, who would be preferred to be called "Barney." Cookie—retired gourmet chef, real name Jack Cook. Then there was retired merchant marine helmsman who, by coincidence, was named Helmsman and called Helm for short. Then last if I forgot to mention, was Captain Dick Mobley, who just preferred to be called Captain or just Cap.

All this came down in the first log I took on my first journey with Captain Mobley down under. He encouraged me to write that first log. He said all mariners kept logs of their journeys, something to look back on and build memories. He said he and his crew, as he referred to them, would all like a log for their own. I agreed.

From that point on, Captain always called his crew his boys, men, crew, guys, etc., and didn't refer each by name. This is what the crew preferred. He called me James, and it stuck. I said I would also call him Captain or Cap out of respect for his position because that was drilled into me—military protocol.

When that journey was over (and what a journey it was!), I thought, *Well, that's it*. Now as I lay in my bunk tonight, I realize he has talked me into three journeys, and now this is the fourth! By the time I get this fourth log finished for him, I will have writer's cramp! And also, James, if you don't stop rattling your thoughts and go to sleep, you will be another victim of Cookie's pan!

Chapter 6

Dawn came early! This was the big day of Captain Mobley's surprise trip and treat for his crew and also me as a guest! I tried to hurry but, somehow, I was a little late for breakfast. When I walked in the galley, all hands were at the table. The crew went, "Hooah!"

Captain was laughing, and Cookie, with hands on hips and one eyebrow cocked, was staring me down. Wow, I felt so small! They were all snickering now.

"I'm sorry, boys. I did try my best! Does this mean I get a bad mark?"

Captain replied, "No, James. You don't get a bad mark! We all have done it a time or two!" The guys were all chuckling and going on with conversation, and Cookie was serving me up with a smile. I felt relieved!

Captain went on to say he had a bus scheduled for the day. We are all going to have a tour of Singapore, then a lunch at the best restaurant, and then the big bonanza—a tour of Singapore's new spectacular indoor gardens! The crew was excited to be catered to like this.

Well, the tour of Singapore itself was spectacular! And almost an all-day affair. When we got to the botanical gardens, we could not believe our eyes! It was huge, all encased in a glass atrium. You rode through in an electric tram. Very quiet, very easy, and comfortable. The interior had every part of nature that you would ever want to see.

Waterfalls, streams, rock formations, all species of blooming flowers, all plant life including mature trees, all species of birds, free and singing, other wildlife, monkeys in the trees, fish in the streams, and too much more for me to even mention. You lost track that you were even riding! It was so spectacular that you were totally unaware that you were moving. So awe-inspiring that you could not get your mind wrapped around it!

On the bus back to the ship, you did not hear a sound. Everyone was lost in their thoughts! When we got to the ship, the crew thanked Captain for such a wonderful day, a day that they would never forget!

The sun was setting, and Captain said, "Tomorrow is another day."

So the crew knew that we would not be getting under-way early or not at all! They all headed for their bunks, relieved and happy!

"Let's sit a while before we turn in, James." So we sat for a long time in silence. Finally, he asked, "Do you have a pretty place in the States?"

"Yes, I do, Cap, but I had hard work—and twenty-five years of it—to develop 158 acres. Folks around there said I had a paradise. Well, yes, I had a beautiful place that Anita and I transformed, but I wouldn't say a paradise."

There was silence for a while, then he spoke, "You know, on the outback with thousands of acres on your sta-tion with cattle, you are not going to develop much. But the land around the homestead is planted grass, trees, and flowers. Sheila built raised beds. All this flourished because of the deep well water supply. With the hep on the station, we could keep everything beautiful."

After a pause, Captain continued, "Well, James, what did you think of the botanical gardens today?"

"Well, Cap, I thought or felt like maybe the garden of Eden would be like that, only more spectacular. We must remember that man was responsible to make those beautiful gardens, but there is no way to compare what was created in the heavens."

Captain went on to say, "Yes, I have viewed those gardens twice now. Yes, some would say it is a paradise—yes, a man-made paradise, but no comparison to the real." Captain was silent for a time, a concerned look upon his face. I waited for him to speak again. "James, do you think I will ever go to paradise?

Wow. I was silent for a moment, and then I said, "Captain, I'm not a preacher man! Most of them think they know, but they, too, are just men quoting their ideas. Do I ever think you will get to paradise? Cap, I don't even know if I will! But let me say this: you believe in the same Creator that I believe in, the one that has created all these wonderful things on earth that we enjoy. We are to be good stewards of what we are given. I would say that you have been a good steward and respectful of all nature on land and on the sea. You have loved and helped all people in need. You are a kind and considerate man for all people. You have always served your best.

"Will you and I get to paradise? I hope and pray we will! We need to take our hope and combine it with faith. Add in love, for hope, faith, and love in our Creator is the best answer I can give. And that is all he wants in return for all he has given. I hope that this has not offended you. That's the best answer I can give!"

There was silence for a very long time now. I knew Captain was seeking answers in his mind!

I knew we should turn in now, but I wasn't going to make a move and disturb his thoughts. Finally, he stood up. He shook his head. He walked over to me, and I could see the mist in his eyes. He smiled and gave me one of his big bear hugs!

"Thanks, James, for giving me hope! The faith and love I have already put into practice!"

Chapter 7

"Well, the next stop is Japan, right, Captain?"

"Yes, and let me tell you why. I have a friend up there by the name of Darrel Ying."

"Wait a minute, Captain. Ying is a Chinese name!"

He chuckled and went on. "Yes, it is. But, you see, his father's name was Ying. Darrel had a Chinese father and a Japanese mother. She was a Fujiyama. When Darrel's father died, she took back her maiden name. If you question Darrel, he gets upset and says that he is Japanese! Sometimes, to rattle his cage, I'll call him Ying Yang! Then he will reverse my name and say, 'Mobley Dick!' You know, like Moby Dick! Then I'll say, 'No, I'm Captain Ahab!' And he laughed. We don't mean it in a bad way. It's just a thing we do."

"Yes, I know. Anita and I had a thing! At bedtime, I would say, 'Goodnight, Dick,' and she would say, 'Good night, Dick.' Something the Smother Brothers would do at the end of their show!"

"Well," he went on. "Darrel caught wind of me coming this way, and he insisted for me to bring you and come for a visit. So we will honor the old gent and go for dinner and a chat!"

I said nothing.

Captain went on. "You will see that he is a gracious host and a rich man at that! He lives on Osaka, in the lower islands of Japan. He owns quite a bit of land. His farm is terraced, and he grows all types of fruits and vegetables to export and also to send through the islands.

"At the bottom of his terrace, he has a large acreage that he irrigates and grows rice. This is also exported.

"Some of the help are fishermen, and they harvest all sorts of seafood from the sea and export them. All the rage now is sea urchins. The divers go down to the sea bottom to harvest them, then they, too, are processed and shipped to the major cities of Japan, where they are in demand!

"He has started another produce—teriyaki sauce.

"Now I'll mention that, and let's see his response." Then Captain chuckled but wouldn't let on. "So, James, after this visit, I suspect you will have a full load for your log!"

When we got to the Japanese islands, approaching from the south, it was a beautiful sight! When we approached the island, there was a natural waterway that led into the inland sea. Then a short course north to Osaka! When we left, it would be the same route back to the Pacific. The only passage to the inland sea.

What a place, I thought. All the homes along the shoreline had terraced gardens down to the sea, beautiful flowers, plants, and crops, and the sea to gather more to eat. We moved into a pier that belonged to Darrel. After we were secured, he gave the crew shore leave until nightfall. Darrel had a driver waiting to transport us to his home, which in itself was spectacular.

His estate was very big and ran from the top of the mountain to the shore of the sea. His property was also terraced and had various crops growing, and at the bottom, I saw the huge rice field he irrigated to grow his crop for export. He welcomed us in at his door. Introductions were made and, right away, I could see why Captain Mobley admired him as a friend.

I was fascinated with the walls that looked like parchment paper. Large panels that could be pushed aside and opened up! He led us to a room that had a floor so elegant that I thought it had to be the ancient sandalwood they talked about. It shined like a mirror. His table was teakwood and also glowed and had rattan placemats.

The table was very short-legged so that you had to sit cross-legged or half-recline on the mats.

It was just us in the room. His wife was out of sight, as was the custom. Darrel clapped his hands, and a young girl came in and bowed. She was a beautiful girl, dressed in native clothing and looked like a geisha girl. Darrel spoke softly to her. She nodded and bowed! In a matter of minutes, she came back with a serving cart with our dinner and set things on the table. Chopsticks were placed beside the dish of Darrel and Captain Mobley, and a fancy spoon beside mine. I thought, *How elegant.* He already knew I probably could not handle chopsticks!

Darrel spoke, "I hope tonight's meal is satisfactory, James? It is succulent pork braised and cooked well-done, mixed into bean sprouts, water chestnuts, bamboo shoots, and snow peas, mixed in a special sauce and served with white rice."

"It is actually my favorite, Mr. Ying."

"No 'Mr.' You call me Darrel!" Then he said, "And also here is my special teriyaki sauce, if you wish!"

I looked over at Captain and saw the grin on his face. I knew what was coming, and I said to myself, "Oh brother!"

Captain Mobley then spoke up with the biggest grin on his face! "So how is the new enterprise coming along, Darrel?" And he pointed to the teriyaki sauce.

Darrel sat silent for a moment or two, then looked at me! "I have named my sauce 'Yang's Teriyaki Sauce' in honor of this bloke sitting beside me!"

And Captain burst out in a big laughing fit, and soon, Darrel was laughing so hard he had tears. That did it for me—I had to join in!

After we regained some composure, Darrel started again, "The teriyaki sauce is doing quite well, my friend, with your name on it!" Another round of serious laughter!

All tension gone, and everybody was happy!

Dinner was delicious. Then the pretty girl came silently back and quietly removed the dishes. There was a pause, and then she came back with hot tea and carafe of sake. Darrel took a teaspoon and put a teaspoonful in his tea. "Gentlemen, help yourself. A little sake in the tea is good for the heart and mind."

Then it was talk time, and we talked and told stories to a late hour. Then Darrel summoned his driver to take us back to the ship. In departing, he said, "Gentlemen, this has been so enjoyable and refreshing. We must all get together again."

And Captain Mobley, wanting to get in the last word, said, "And Darrel, thank you for naming the sauce!" And more laughter as we departed! Captain remarked, "Wonderful man!"

Getting underway in the morning, we left the beauty of Osaka, rounded the inland sea, and out the passage.

Captain was at the wheel with Helmsman standing by. "Captain, do you want me to take watch?"

"No, James. We have a long journey ahead. Good time for you to catch up your log."

"Thanks, Cap." So I returned to my guest cabin and contemplated what to write.

Japan covers more than two thousand miles, consisting of thousands of islands. The north island barely touches the large center island. Then next is the large southern island with many outcrops and many, many small islands. It is bordered by the Pacific Ocean on the east and the Sea of Japan on the west. They contain the natural beauty of an area still being formed—smoking volcanos, many hotspots, and deep running streams, cliffs rising beside the sea.

Japan in its lifetime has endured earthquakes, volcanic eruptions, tsunamis, landslides, typhoons, floods—not to mention the calamities of war! But the people have prevailed. They have riches from the sea, terraced slopes that allow them gardens and crops. From the peaks and valleys, they have built homes, gardens, terraces, and in larger areas, cities, industrial sites, and sites of technology and advancing training and educational centers that have enhanced their lifestyle.

And I'll never forget the pass through the waterway to the inland sea, the beauty of Osaka, and a visit with Darrel Ying, a fluent businessman and a longtime friend of Captain Mobley!

Chapter 8

When we broke into the Pacific and took our bearing north in open waters, Captain said we were in for a long stretch. He said he would try to stay coastal to break the monotony of the water and hope for a smoother passage. We would lay over near the coast of Asia and Siberia, that was so, Captain said, "The Russians don't get us!" Then he chuckled.

You never know! But I bet the captain would give a good fight. Maybe not a winner but a last good go. With all the fishing boats that traveled the area, we may have been well under the radar!

After so many sea days and sea nights, we were traveling close to the Asian-Siberian side of the Pacific! Helm at the wheel, and Captain on close watch. We were approaching an area called Kurk Island that didn't look like an island because it was so close to the shore. Captain, in his glass, turned and pointed to the individual on the shore. It looked like an Indian sitting by a fire with his boat beached.

"Stand down and slow down, crew. I want to make contact with that man. Pull in down slow and drop anchor." Which we did, all executed well-done.

"Sit here a piece and let him get a good look at us and generate a little curiosity! Don't want to scare him off!" We waited for a spell, and the old Indian never attempted to leave, but he wasn't going to move either.

Captain said, "We could lower our small boat and go to him, but that might scare him off. Everybody, wave like you're trying to wave him into us. That we don't intend to go to him!" We did that for a while with no result!

So Captain said, "Helm, you know a little bit of Russian, don't you?"

"Not pure Russian, but a little Slavic Russian."

"Call to him. See if he understands."

So Helm did the best he could with broken Russian. Directly, the old Indian got up and headed for his boat. He pushed off and started toward us. The crew dropped a rope ladder over the side, and he kept coming, us waving him in.

When he got to the ladder, Helm kept encouraging him with his Slavic Russian. Up the ladder he came. Helm asked him in Russian if he could speak English. He grinned. "Yes, I speak Indian, English, and better Russian than you do!"

Then Helm asked, "You know we mean no harm. Peaceful."

The old Indian looked up and pointed to flags. "Two good countries I saw, and I had no fears."

Captain Mobley said, "We thought you might be a little knowledgeable about the Aleutians? Are we near? Are they inhabited?"

The old Indian said, "You are very near the tip of the islands, and yes, the Aleut Indians inhabit some of the islands. Your government established a wildlife sanctuary on one larger and a wildlife preserve on another. The Aleut, by a different name, crossed from here when it was still a land. Then the water rose, and we have islands.

"They hunt, fish, and live off the land in the old way. They make boats and sleds to travel winter and summer!"

We were kind of awestruck, so we said nothing.

"Do you want to hear legend handed down to me?"

"Yes," said Captain.

He pointed back to his fire. "Years ago, my grandfather sat right there. So here I now have my fire. He was approached by a man in strange clothes, clothes he had made, boots he had made. He told Grandfather that he was a military flyer and was shot down by Russians in a neutral fly zone. They captured him and imprisoned him. The Russian commander told him he had to go on air and denounce his country. He said he would not. The Russians said you will be imprisoned for life. The flyer said he was raised Apache Indian, and he was Apache, and yes, one day, he would escape!

"The commander called for his tracker to come in. He was a Siberian Indian. The two Indians looked at each other. The Russian said to the Apache, 'You will never escape because my tracker is the best in Siberia, and he knows the land.'

"One day, the Apache escaped. He traveled into Siberia. It may have been a year he was in the wilderness. The Siberian Indian was in hot pursuit. The flyboy's clothes wore out. He made bow and arrow like forefathers. He killed game and used the hides to make Indian clothes. He ate from forest and drank from streams. He was always just one step ahead of the Siberian tracker! They had the whole army in pursuit.

"Once they spotted him and set the helicopter down, he killed the crew with his bow and arrow and destroyed the aircraft. He traveled for a year across Siberia using his nature skills and sense of direction. One night, he came here—this very place! He told my grandfather his story by the fire. My grandfather was afraid of this Indian. He told Grandfather not to fear. His people came from Grandfather's people centuries ago, when the islands were land.

"'We are brothers. I want to buy your boat. I must cross the water at these islands and get back to my people.'

"Grandfather said, 'You will never make it. The radar covers the islands.'

"He said, 'I will travel at night and stay low under the radar. Sell me your boat.'

"Grandfather said, 'I will not be here tonight, but my boat will be here for you!' That night, the Siberian tracker came. There was a great fight. The Apache was strong by a year in the wild. The fight was hard and long.

"Grandfather came back in the morning to check! His boat was gone. He found the Siberian Indian. He was dead! He had been scalped!"

We stood there in awe! What a story. One of the crew asked, "Did he make it?"

The Indian looked at him and nodded his head. "Yes. Word came back through over Indian pipeline. The Apache got back to his people!"

Then he said, "Soon you will see the Aleutians, and the people you see will be my people from long ago! Be kind to my people. And one more thing. Are you going on to Alaska?"

Captain said, "Yes."

"One more thing," the Indian said. "Many years ago, when the Russians were taking over Alaska, a ship came, like yours. Its flag was big like the little corner in your flag. He was English. He was kind to the Indians, treated them well. They say his name was Cook!"

Captain and I looked at each other, and our mouths dropped! "Did you know he was here?" I asked.

"No," said Captain. "I thought he got as far as Hawaii and was killed! I'll check it out when we reach Alaska!"

Cookie disappeared for a moment, then reappeared with something wrapped in cheesecloth. He handed it to the Indian. He smelled it and grinned. It was down the rope ladder he went, and we watched him go ashore. He pulled his boat up into the beach, kicked out his fire, and disappeared into the underbrush.

Captain asked, "Cookie, what was it you gave him?"

"Smoked salmon," said Cookie.

"That wasn't my dinner you gave away, was it?" Captain said.

"No," said Cookie with a sheepish look. "Our supper is ready!"

"What are we having, Cookie?"

"Well, it's a pot of navy beans with a little salt pork added."

"Wow," said Captain, "so much for a gourmet cook!"

I spoke up, "Make it soup. I like navy bean soup. Mom used to make it for us boys, and it was so good!"

Crewman Ned spoke up. "Cookie, can you throw a little ham in it?"

"Can do!"

Captain looked at me, and I said, "All good, Cap. When you deal with an Indian for material or advisement, the person who is asking is required to give one small gift to whoever he is dealing with. For instance, I had an Indian come to me to ask me if he could buy my property. To negotiate, he brought me a little homemade pouch full of tobacco. That would be his gift to open talks."

"Well, did you sell it to him for a sack of tobacco?"

"No, Cap. He wanted to pay me so much by the month to buy the property. I said no. I couldn't do that because I need the money to buy another property."

"So, James, what was your bottom line?"

"My bottom line was, 'No wampun, no campun!'"

Everybody got their laugh out of that one!

Cookie said, "Do you want me to bang the pan? Or do you guys want cold beans?"

Everybody hustled for the galley!

On the way, Captain said, "I don't want leftovers for breakfast!"

We were hungry, and we plowed into the beans, and they were really good. Cookie had laced them with ham, as requested. Captain announced, "We are already anchored and secure. We will stay for the night. We can pull out at daylight."

Jake piped up, "What if the Russians come?"

Captain said, "We'll feed them beans." Then he roared with laughter. So everybody got their input today, and it was a good day all around, even with the beans!

Chapter 9

No cold beans for breakfast. Cookie put on a good meal. Captain just smiled! Time to pull anchor and resume our journey. That we did, and in a short time, the Aleutians were in sight. We felt our goal had been met. Now for a sail through and a look over.

Captain said, "James, is there something you can write on this?"

"Sure, Cap. Will tell about the islands, what the Indian referred to, and don't forget we have to pick upon Captain James Cook!"

"Right," he said.

Cookie was taking all this in, and when our conversation came to a pause, he came over to Captain Mobley and I. He looked at us sheepishly and said, "Captain, I need to apologize for the beans! I really should have done better, but with all the excitement about the Indian, I lost track of time and just got up a quick supper. I'm embarrassed. You are right. Beans from a gourmet cook?"

Captain patted Cookie on the shoulder, and said, "Jack", and that was the first time I ever heard Captain call Cookie by his first name! Jack Cook! And so Captain said, "Jack, you are not to worry about that. I was just having a little fun putting you on. As a matter of fact, those beans were the best I ever had. I ate two bowls! They were gourmet beans! So in the future, if it calls for a good round of them again, let's go for it!"

Cookie was relieved, and he joked back, "Well, I didn't want you to put me on the shore with that kind old Indian and leave me!"

Captain threw back his head and had a hearty laugh! "Cookie, you're not getting away from me that easy. This ship could not run without your cooking! Anyhow, I thought that was a nice gesture, you giving him the salmon wrapped in cheesecloth. Kinda like they do things."

"And when I did that, did you notice what he did?"

"No," we said.

He pulled some stones out of his pocket and showed us. "He gave me these stones!" They were round and polished from the continual washing and smoothing by the waves of the Pacific.

I looked and said, "Wow, Cookie. He gave you agates."

"What are agates?" he asked.

"Prizes, Cookie. Prizes found only on the Pacific coastline. I hunted them off the Pacific coast of Canada when I was there. People polish them more if not enough and make jewelry!"

Cookie looked at them in his hand and said, "That good ole Indian gave me something valuable, didn't he?"

"Yes, he did. And now what are you going to do with them?"

He stared at the stones. "I'm going to have these made into jewelry for Simone!"

Captain then remarked, "Now there couldn't be a better memory of the Aleutians than that! Every time you look at them, you will remember when and where and how you acquired them on this voyage. All for your kindness with a small piece of smoked salmon!"

We were getting first good sight of the island, and Captain cried out, "Land ho!"

And all the crew became alert to start watching and viewing the dream we had come for. The first land in the north that they had never seen before. The same land that their hero, Captain James Cook, had passed through centuries ago!

"Are we going to port here?" I asked.

"No, we are going to take the day and the next to slowly idle by and take it all in! I'm not sure of the waters, and on the far side you can see the Bering Sea. I'm not too anxious to move into those waters. Like the old Indian said, 'Don't disturb my people!' I will pay respect to that."

Yes, these are his people. People that crossed centuries ago. People who are alert now, but in different times, they crossed a land mass and evolved into hundreds of different tribes that we know today. Now the Aleuts are living on these islands that once was a solid land mass from one side to another.

"James! Seize the moment! We are looking at history centuries old! No, we will not disturb these people! We have achieved what we came for—the quest to see the Aleutians!"

I stood spellbound as Captain spoke of this. It was coming straight from his heart.

Captain, manning his ship, stayed mindful of the depths of the water and tacked as close to the shoreline as possible. Some of the people on shore stopped what they were doing and stared at the ship. A ship that no longer plowed these waters. What was on their minds? The ancients return?

You could see movement of people on the shore up.

Up ahead was the wildlife sanctuary that the old Indian spoke about. Some more islands and then a larger island where the game reserve was located.

Moving on, we were moving up the coast of the peninsula of Alaska. Captain looked at me. "James, do we have words to write about this?"

"Yes, I have words. Also researched a little before we came! What is amazing is that what it tells us is we have just passed, not the modern part, but the primitive part.

"What it tells is what we see now in the Aleuts. Their way of life and ways that have been handed down from the peoples that crossed this landmass centuries ago. And also, some history on your favorite—Captain James Cook!"

Aleutian Islands, Alaska—home of the Aleut people. Bordered by the Bering Sea on the north and the Pacific on the south. The chain of islands, most named, some not. Centuries ago, the chain was connected by one continuous landmass until the waters of the Pacific rose to create islands.

When it was a continual landmass, historians say that the first Indians crossed this landmass from Siberia and started to populate the country now called America. They spread north to the far reaches of the north and south to

Mexico and beyond. Tribes became many by name, and all of the continent was covered with Indian tribes, as well as the ones who moved toward Alaska and Canada.

Alaska was inhabited for thousands of years by various native groups, each having their own culture and language. To talk about all the tribes that populated Alaska and Canada would take volumes in itself, so let me give a little history on two tribes that inhabited the Aleutian chain centuries ago, since our goal is to cover the islands and part of Alaska on this cruise.

The Aleuts, name fitting, settled the windswept Aleutian chain ten thousand years ago. Their location allowed them to harvest the sea's bounty, but they also had to contend with the harvest and unpredictable weather as well as earthquakes and volcanic eruptions. They had learned how to make various nets, hooks, and lines. They used the nets and lines to capture sea lions and sea otters. Then they used a stone-bladed lance.

Their women and children gathered shellfish at low tide, another staple. Because of their dependence on the sea, they rarely traveled inland. They did develop an ingenious method of traveling over the snow. They made skis by drying seal skin and covering it over wooden frames. This gave them travel aid, much like the modern skis.

Their warm clothing was made from sea lion skins, complete with fur collars and hoods. They used body material from the sea lions to also cover the front of their sleds to keep the driver dry. In the summer, with grass so plentiful, the Aleut women would weave baskets—some mats and clothing were also made in the same way.

The Alutiiqs were close relatives to the Aleuts. They settled on the Alaska Peninsula, Kenai Peninsula, and Prince William Sound, dating back seven thousand years. They were skilled maritime hunters and fishers. They also hunted sea lions, seals, sea otters, and even whales. They fished for halibut, cod, and salmon. Also they harvested sea birds and their eggs. Occasionally they hunted bears and caribou.

The people collected all manner of items to make their clothes, homes, and tools. Animal skins, feathers, bones, sod, drifted wood, grasses. Many houses were made of sod and partly dug into the ground. These were often reinforced with whale bones or driftwood. Seal oil was used to light their lamps!

Then the Russian invasion came in 1741, when two small vessels, the *St. Peter* and *St. Paul*, captained by a Dane, Vitus Bering, and, Russian, Alexei Chirikov, that started off the first encounter and drew interest from the Russians. They wanted the wealth that Alaska had to offer, so it was takeover, and Russia dominated the land for years.

As we read down through history, it was a wrestling match between Russia and the US for possession!

Finally, it became and American buyout, and later it became the forty-ninth state of the Union.

About the time prior, when all this involvement with Russia was going on, the British were continuing their search for the Northwest Passage, the fabled waterway between the Atlantic and Pacific. In 1778, Captain James Cook sailed north from Vancouver Island through the inside passage and then along the Gulf Coast to the Aleutians. Along the way, he explored a narrow embankment that would later be given his name, Cook Inlet.

The Russians tried to impress him with their control over the region, but Cook saw that with how tenuous the position of this group of hunters and traders stationed three thousand miles from their homeland was, there was no threat. Although Cook died in Hawaii after visiting Alaska, his crew continued on to Canton, China, where they sold their Alaskan sea otter pelts for an outlandish price.

Britain became interested and increased their sailing to the northwest coast. Then came the Spanish, who were well-established on the California coast! This piece of history came as a surprise to Captain Mobley. He did not know that Captain Cook had ventured that far north before his death.

We would dock at Kenai, which is a safe harbor, and venture from there. We could take in Anchorage and then north to Fairbanks, taking in all the sights of interest, this time staying at tourist facilities.

From this north point, we looped around south, down to Glenallen, back coming down on south road to Anchorage, and on down to Kenai. We had rented a twelve-passenger van to take this tour. Nobody had to be constantly in the middle and had full visibility from the windows.

Before we started our trip back down, Captain Mobley had asked Helm if he would like him to rent a plane up there, then we could fly on up to the Klondike to look over the gold fields.

There was silence for a moment, then Helm said, "No, I've seen enough dirt and rocks in my time!" Everyone got a good laugh about that!

Back down again to the *Sheila II*, and all hands were tuckered out but well-satisfied with the journey. It was late, and Captain Mobley asked Cookie if this was a good time to throw on another pot of beans tonight. "No!" Cookie exclaimed! "Tonight, we eat at a fancy place on shore, and the treat's on me!" Laughter all around.

Then Captain said, "Sure is good to have a good cook!" Laughter again! Cookie smiled. You just couldn't get one over on the old captain! He had a ready remark for everything.

"Okay, guys," he said. "Good rest tonight. Tomorrow is a free day for all. You might want to go back to Anchorage for a look! Next morning, gents, we get underway! Another long journey down to Hawaii." They all cheered, even though they figured that was in the plans!

"James, you ever been to Hawaii?"

"Yes, Cap, I have. Many years ago."

"Which island should we stop at?"

"Well, Cap, we have a ship to sleep on, so no hotel expense to pay out. Although I would recommend taking our meals at the motels because the food is reasonable and fantastic! With the ship as base, I don't know why we can't hit them all!" The cheer went up. "To go on, I want this to be my treat. It's about time!"

Cookie stood up! "No, James. No expense on you or Captain. I suggest we all chip into a pot! Then as we go along, all expense is drawn on from the pot! If the pot gets low, we chip in again. We keep this going until Fiji or home. Goodness knows all of us here are well-heeled, and it won't hurt us a bit!"

The crew added a yes!

I said, "Okay. That's a plan! The day after tomorrow, we pull out!"

Chapter 10

"D-day" came—that is, the day of departure. We pulled out of safe harbor off the coast of Alaska and headed out into the big Pacific. Thank goodness it had been summer in Alaska! We were Hawaii-bound! I asked Captain, "Do you want a commentary on Hawaii on the way or after we complete the run? Most of it is on Captain Cook."

"Give it to me before, James. I want to go over the connection of Captain Cook's Alaska tour before his death in Hawaii." There was a pause, and then Captain asked, "Do you want to help master the big waters of the Pacific? Or do you want to set course coastal along the States?"

I had a quick answer, but I waited a moment to watch the expression on his face! "I believe we will take the big water instead of the coastal course!"

"Why is that, James?"

"On the coastal, somebody might call me and say I have to come home now, and I am not ready for that!"

Captain threw back his head and roared with laughter! "Well said, mate. Well said!"

The crew looked at us funny, and they could never figure out what me and Captain was about! So big water it was, and course was set for the islands. When we got there, course changes would be in order from island to island. My mind started to wander, and I was formulating what I was going to say.

Captain saw my puzzlement. "James, write about when you were there. Then history of beginnings, and Captain Cook's episodes on the islands. Tell about the people, and then as a wrap, you can tell about our little stint there."

"Captain, if I write all you spoke about, I won't have too much to tell about us."

"Well, that's okay. Folks want to know about what there is to know about the islands, not a bunch of ragtag sailors traveling through!" Then a hardy laugh.

"Okay, Sid, I'll give it a shot, but I don't think we are ragtags—I think we are state of the art."

He shook his head laughing and left me to my chores!

Hawaii islands! The grouping is grouped into the Big Island, Hawaii, Maui, Molokai, Oahu, and Kauai. The five major islands are the ones tourists want to see. There are smaller islands outside the chain like Niʻihau, Lanai, and Kahoʻolawe. There is one island in the smaller chain that no outsiders are permitted to visit unless they are pure Hawaiian (Polynesian). I'll explain later.

When I visited the islands, I had to come by air into Hilo (top west), then we were taken by bus to Honolulu. I must say that Hilo was very beautiful, and I would like to have stayed a little longer, but wheels turn on the tour!

After the sights in Honolulu, taking in Waikiki Beach, Pearl Harbor, and the *Arizona* memorial site, plus tours, good hotel, and excellent food!

We were flown to Maui for the biggest part of our visit.

Our lodging was in timeshare condos. Several tours from there. We were taken to the pineapple farms and ate fresh fruit from the field. We were also taken to the coffee plantation, where the beans were made into Kona Coffee, the best in the world at that time. We were told that the Kona bean was only grown in Hawaii and maybe one other place in the world. I think it was the best coffee that I ever had to drink.

Then we had a short stay at Molokai and Oahu, both excellent hotels, dining, and sights to see. The last stop and short stay was Kauai. I was really impressed with the island. It was small and quaint with a rich history. It was this island that was heavy in traffic when the whalers were hunting whales, seals, and sea lions. The shopping center there had a good quantity and quality of carvings from tusks and bones. Very intricate work! Kauai was the only island that resisted King Kamehameha. I may repeat this in my narrative at risk of repeating myself!

Kauai was the first island that Captain Cook landed on. He spent five days there before they took a short visit to Ni'ihau, where they traded salt and yams for pigs and goats and also water. Captain Cook's second contact with the Hawaiians occurred a year later at Kealakekua on the Big Island. They were having a big festival to honor and worship their god. The natives, seeing the vessels approaching, thought it was Loki himself (their god) returning to the island.

Cook and his crew experienced the greatest welcome in Hawaii's history. The people greeted the ships by the thousands. From the water, surfboards, and from the shore, canoes. To this, Cook wrote, "I have nowhere in this sea seen such a number of people assembled in one place."

Besides the number of canoes, the people on shore covered the beaches, and hundreds were swimming about the ships. When the party was over, and Loki was not Cook—or Cook was not Loki—the Hawaiians became less friendly, and two thousand warriors attacked the landing party. Some five British marines were killed, including Cook himself. He had a burial at sea, in the blue waters of Kealakekua Bay.

So if you wonder whatever happened to Captain James Cook, the British captain that explored and documented all the islands of the South Pacific and then some? It ended right here in the Hawaiian Islands, off the Big Island in the bay!

Before all this came down, there was a dynasty in the islands. It started with a great warrior by the name or Kamehameha. As King Kamehameha set out to conquer all of the islands and bring them under his rule. He secured Maui and Lanai in 1790. He had several rival chiefs killed to gain control of the Big Island. Then he conquered Molokai and Oahu. He made two attempts to invade Kauai but failed.

In 1810, Kauai chief peacefully surrendered his island, and the entire Hawaii kingdom was under one rule, King Kamehameha. Under his rule, trade with the Europeans began. A big demand for sandalwood occurred, and cutting began, which eventually the cutting took the trees to the ground, and the supply exhausted.

Kamehameha succumbed to a lengthy illness and was buried on the Big Island. His bones were buried in a secret place known only to the moon and stars. Historians estimate that he died at sixty years of age. Liholiho, his son, became Kamehameha II, and soon into his rule, which was short. A wife of several of Kamehameha appointed herself as regent or equal ruler. She insisted that Liholiho set down with her at feast, which was prohibited by the gods! And dine with her.

Now that the gods did not punish her, she ordered all the idols and temples to be destroyed with Liholiho's blessing. Without places of worship, the Hawaiians experienced a spiritual vacuum. In 1820, American missionaries arrived from New England aboard the brig *Thaddeus*. They preached in Honolulu and Kona for a one-year trial period. They never left! They did very well. They married Hawaiian royals and governed land and power.

Liholiho and his queen, Kamamalu, died in London of the measles in 1924, hoping to have audience with King George IV. Liholiho's younger brother, Kauikeaouli, became Kamehameha III! And he started a new base of laws patterned after missionary teachings. Christianity became the new religion. Chiefs were converted first, then the population. Under his rule, Lahaina became one of the most vital ports in the Pacific because of the whaling industry.

The history evolved, and many changes took place. The last king died in 1854. The Hawaiian—I don't recall the name of the island—but the story goes: it was the only island left with a pure Hawaiian (Polynesian) people. No one was allowed to visit or reside on the island unless they were pure Polynesian descendants of the original race. I think they could leave the island as long as they did not intermarry or try to bring back an outsider. Is this still in existence today? I don't know. Maybe this, too, is lost?

So this changes our way of thinking about Captain Cook. Not this pure island, but the fact of his ending. We thought he came as far north as the Hawaiian Islands and met his doom. But no, we found proof that he sailed as far as Alaska, helping Britain search for the Northwest passage, which was never found. Then a year later, he is back again in Hawaii where he meets his doom!

It makes me wonder how communications were carried out! Also, there was no recorded documentation saying his sister ship was with him, so it had to be after that ship's captain and officers were put adrift and took over the ship. I will discuss this with Captain Mobley after we get to Hawaii. Right now, he is busy at the wheel, and I don't want to be a distraction. His knowledge may reveal something and maybe it will not. We go by what was written down in history, and that's that. But there is a lot to the history of these discoverers that we will never know.

Right now, we will be looking for the lower island of the Hawaiian chain!

Chapter II

The first one to cry out, "Land ho!" was Helm. He was watching intently for the signs of the island. From this distance, it was a look of beautiful tropical islands, not one covered with high-rise building and traffic.

Thinking back to World War II, which is not a good thought, my big brother, Tim, was on the Hawaiian Islands, as well as the Philippines. He said then that the islands were purely tropical and beautiful. No improvements! But I know that the islands are shore-to-shore pushing modern cities almost. I wonder what keeps them afloat with all the building weight? Was this ever considered? The experts say the islands are slowly sinking into the sea, yet there are more volcano eruptions? And the islands sit over a fault line between two major plates in the bottom of the sea.

I mentioned to Captain Mobley about my thoughts.

And he said, "Not to worry, James. We will be out of here before all that starts!" Then he went to chuckling.

The ole bugger has an answer for everything! I was thinking, *Yeah, Chicken Little, the sky is falling!*

The journey from Alaska down to the Hawaiian Islands gave us a feel how the journey to Captain Cook must have felt. But his ship was more primitive than ours on the *Endeavor*. Don't get me wrong, the *Endeavor* was a fine ship in its day, and all the controls aboard were top of the line. The controls on all the rigging and maneuvering were top of the line, but it took a big crew to make things work. Probably no gourmet cook either. Probably a goodly ration of salt pork. History says he traded for pigs and goats on one island. Makes me think a little goat was on the diet too!

I turned back to Captain and asked, "Do you want me to take the wheel for a spell, Cap?"

"Sure. Day is good, and sea running smooth. You can take the wheel, and we will reminisce back on things."

So this we did, back to the first journey when we got together. And the following journey. The funny things and the serious things. When you put this altogether, it made good conversation and kept old memories ever-present in our minds. It was a long run down, but time did pass rather quickly.

A shout rang out, "Land ho!" and it was Helm spotting land this time. We knew he was watching intently, anxious for the next excitement of the journey. So we were looking at Kauai, when we were running north to south. It sure looked like a tropical island from a distance until we got closer and saw all the modern structures coming into view.

All the islands were nice at that, even though modern- ization took place. It was still tropical with a nice tempera- ture and winds. Sometimes they have a shower every day during certain seasons but quickly over, and everything is fresh and smelling good.

"We will get there early eve," said Captain. "Good place for a rest and a day ashore."

So that was the plan. A day or so at each island and move up—or should I say down? I guess we will be moving from the smallest to the largest! This little island was a footprint of the others. It had a lot to offer in sights. Hotels were top of the line; their meals were also. Open to the public with a fee, that is. Most hotels at all islands included meals in their package price.

So a night and a day, and we moved on and made port in Oahu. It was a little larger but offered the same as Kauai. We took two days here, and everyone could eat the fabulous meals. Fresh pineapple from the fields, fresh coconut and, of course, fresh poi, which was a Hawaiian staple. You could have one-finger, two-finger, or three-finger poi, if you really thought you wanted it!

Also there were the shows, the hula girls in grass skirts, and as we moved into the larger islands, more and more to see. Like I mentioned before at Lahaina, the ivory carvings history about the sailing ships making port. Many shops, Kona coffee plantation, volcano tour, diamond head, black sand beach, a tour on the Big Island, where they took you to the only cattle ranch in Hawaii that had a large operation and raised purebred Santa Gertrudis cattle for breeding stock and also for market.

Another attraction, the Punch Bowl cemetery, a dormant volcano, where thousands of military service boys and girls are buried from World War II and, of course, Pearl Harbor and the USS *Arizona* Memorial.

I bounced through the islands and gave you this input in order not to repeat at each island. Most islands are alike when it comes to entertainment.

As we progressed through Molokai, Maui, and the Big Island of Hawaii, it was like turning kids loose at a circus with the crew. They had to see everything, taste everything, and do everything. And one of our highlights was being invited to a pig roast by a major hotel. The managers had seen us at dock. They came down to see the ship, and Captain Mobley took them on tour! They had never seen a sailing ship pull in!

A pig roast was a pit dug in the ground and a large amount of coals built and burnt in the bottom. Then palm leaves were covered over the coals. Then the pig was lowered down on the palm leaves. More palm leaves covered the pig, and the pit was covered with earth. At the prescribed time, the earth is removed, the top palms removed, and the pig removed and served!

I don't think Cap and crew or I missed any sights or sounds that had to be had, so we went island to island, took our time, and stayed long enough to take it all in.

Captain Mobley was in a hurry. They had never hit these islands before because they always heard they were too modern, too overbuilt. But no, there's more to see and do than meets the eye!

When we pulled into Port Molokai, Maui, and the Big Island Hawaii, we became an added attraction. People were fascinated to see this big sail ship pull in and dock! When we disembarked, the people crowded around Captain and crew (incidentally, the crew had been wearing their old-fashioned uniforms while visiting the islands).

They wanted to know if this was a cruise ship. And could they book a cruise?

The captain took a stand! "No, folks, this is not a cruise ship per se, and no, you cannot book on. But I can give you folks a better deal! I have a friend by the name of Curt, who has a completely restored de Havilland seaplane. Seats twenty people! I have his phone number! He is based down in American Samoa! For a phone call and a fee, which is more reasonably than the air flights here from island to island, he will pick you up and fly you to any island you want.

"Plus he stays on and waits for you! All the major air-lines have to gain an altitude of two thousand feet before they descend to the next airfield. Curt doesn't need an air-field. He lands on water, docks, and loads. Besides, he is not restricted to the two thousand feet airspace. He can fly island to island, low, and show you all the sights. Who wants his number?"

Everybody wanted that number, and this was a repeat performance for the next three major islands! Captain about gave me writer's cramp, writing down all these num-bers on little pieces of paper!

"And, oh! Folks, if he asks you where you got your information, you tell him Captain Mobley gave it to you!" Then he chuckled, and the show was over!

Then we and crew took in our show on those three major islands. We had our fun. Now it was time to head home. We had permission to dock at Pearl Harbor. It was kind of a solemn departure, considering the memorial and all.

On the way out and turning south setting course, I asked Captain, "Wonder what old Curt is going to think when all those calls come in?"

Captain went to chuckling. "Well, ole Curt will have all the business he wants!" Then Captain couldn't help but laugh! "You know, ole Curt and his buddy may have to hurt up and restore another one of those planes!"

We went through the watches with Cap, Helm, and I. Easy time. Then as we were going along, Captain looked down at his instruments and reached up and rang a bell furiously! A cheer went up from the crew! We were under the equator! We were "down under!"

Captain yelled out, "Who wants a stop at Fiji?"

The cheer went up again! Captain looked at me and smiled. "Well, James, I guess we make our old proverbial stop at Fiji!"

When we get to Fiji, Captain will dock at the same place where he always docks, on the way in. The one that is right at a quaint shopping center. We get a day to go ashore and browse around. The crew buys trinkets for the girls, we rest that night, and get underway in the morning. Sydney is not far off! Going home!

Chapter 12

As we sighted Sydney Harbour, the old proverbial shout rang out! "Thar she blows!" Another traditional thing with the crew. Signaling the end of another cruise, and what a journey it has been! A very long journey to the north lands, but a successful one at that. No mishaps, smooth sailing, taking in ocean territory that they have never invaded before.

You could see the feelings all around. A tinge of regret for journey's end, but that happy feeling, good to be home. We had docking and securing and cleanup to do in one day, off tomorrow, before the girls came the next. That was another tradition. When we came back from a cruise, the girls were home. Girls meaning wives and sweethearts. That day was party day, and we celebrated all day. Good talk, good food, and no booze! The girls told their adventures while we were gone, and we told ours.

Captain Mobley at the helm, we approached *Sheila II*'s berth, and Captain slipped her in nice and easy. A small bump off the protection fenders. The crew went into action fast, pulling out the downs, and the dockhands jumped in to help! All laughter and cutting up all around.

Now it was time to lay back and rest until our one day off tomorrow before the girls arrived. That day was spent on ship's cleanup fore and aft! Cookie was busy in the galley, keeping us fed and preparing tomorrow's menu for the festivities, and tomorrow passed fast.

The third day, here come the girls like they were unleashed from somewhere! They ran to their respective mates, and it was hugs and kisses, welcome home safe and sound. I stood by as usual, then out of the crowd, Leilani came forward and wrapped her arms around me and laid a big kiss on my lips! I was dumbfounded. That happened last cruise when she came to tell me she knew I was in and had volunteered for my flight leaving out.

Leilani was a flight attendant on Qantas Air.

Captain Mobley looked over at me with a big grin! "Well, James. I hope you won't get mad at me! I contacted Leilani and told her you were in! I invited her to join us!"

"How could I get mad? A beautiful girl from Samoa who is giving me all her attention."

As she was hanging on like I was going to run, I thought of what Captain Mobley and I discussed the last time. He said, "James, you need a good woman. It has been long enough!"

I returned with, "But, Captain, we are two worlds apart!

Leilani lives down under, and I live above the equator! Also, she is a pretty young thing in the beginning of her lifetime, and I'm moving into the end of my lifetime." But I said to myself, "If I were just forty years younger, there is no doubt that I would propose to Leilani—without a doubt!"

So for now the two of us joined the celebration as a couple! The contact became important to me! Near the end of the day, it was time for us to both leave. When the time drew nigh, I picked up my gear and took Leilani by the hand and headed for the gangway. All activity stopped, and the folks came forward to bid us goodbye.

I said, "Leilani, take my left hand, for I need my right!" Stepping on the gangway, still holding hands, I turned aft and executed a sharp salute to the flag. I then turned to Captain Mobley and snapped him a salute! "Permission to leave the ship, sir?"

"Permission granted, Officer James." Then handshakes and hugs came from all around. It was emotional for me. I never liked goodbyes! A cab was waiting and whisked Leilani off to the airport. We separated, and she went on to prepare for her flight duties.

I checked in and found a seat to wait for boarding call.

As I moved up the stairs to board, Leilani was in the receiving line. As I approached her, she winked and said, "Good evening, Mr. James!"

I settled into my seat—which was two. I always purchased a second seat so I could be alone. This was in first class. Leilani gave instructions to ready for takeoff.

The flight captain came on and announced, "Folks, we have fog closing in over Sydney Bay. Not to worry, we will soon be above and into clear and sunny skies!"

Once we were off, Leilani came and buckled into my spare seat. My cellphone rang! "James! This is Captain

Mobley. So sorry, mate! The bay is socked in with fog, and we won't be able to take the *Sheila II* out and give you a sendoff!"

I answered, "No problem, mate. Put your phone on visual chat, and everybody gather round. This is my go, Cap!" I saluted into the cellphone, and everybody saluted back!

Leilani called into her mic, "Captain, wobble your wings! Now!"

Captain replied, "What for? It is pea soup down here!"

"Just do it!" she yelled.

So he wobbled the wings twice. I shouted to Captain, "Can you see the plane?"

"Yes, we all did, mate! Good to ya!" We could see and hear the whole group waving and laughing.

"You tell the crew and all! I love you guys! Hang loose 'til we meet again."

Leilani had to get up and take her duties. She bent down and brushed a light kiss on my cheek. "Good go, James!"

As she walked away, I said, "I have my log! You will get a copy. I have your address!"

Leilani replied, "I will be counting on that, and I also want you to stay in touch!"

"Yes, will do."

Now like on the other flights, darkness settled in as we moved through the time zones. I guess I drifted off to sleep again. I thought I heard a rustle. That brought me awake. "That you, Skipper? How are things in paradise?"

"Extremely beautiful, but so lonesome without you!"

"I know, baby, but time will tell when I can come to you!"

"I see Leilani has settled in for the night, peaceful on your shoulder! I think she is getting pretty attached!"

I stayed quiet—didn't answer! Silence for a while, then more conversation. "Well, I guess I shouldn't blame you! You have had a very long run of being alone. Do you still love me?"

"Yes, baby. I still love you. Always will, no matter what!"

"James, that makes me feel good to hear that!"

I stayed quiet for a moment, then asked, "Skipper, does that mean I don't get a bad mark this time?"

"No, baby. You don't get a bad mark this time! It has been going on five years now that I left you. I can understand your loneliness! I'm surprised that you haven't moved on!"

"Only because of love being strong, and you would be hard to replace!"

"I'm glad you didn't find another, but I did leave you with a lot of loneliness and no happiness!"

"Honey, do you think I'll be able to be with you?"

"I think I recall you having a talk with Captain Mobley about that? You and Captain took that little journey to the gardens at Singapore! I think you both are on the right track! You both got a taste of paradise at the gardens, but I can assure you, sweetheart, it is much better than that. In the world, people sometimes think that life will go on forever, but in reality, there is no forever there! The world is time-bound. So there is, yes, an end to things.

"Paradise is the real forever! There is no time in paradise because it is eternal.

"So on earth, when you say, 'I'll love you forever' or 'I'll never leave you,' it's just a figure of speech! It will become real in paradise! Captain Mobley can cling to the good ship called hope. You and Captain Mobley are on the right course. Hope and faith! I have to go now, love. I'll say good night."

"Good night, Skipper. And yes, I'll love you forever!"

Odyssey
Down Under

Part V

Return to Fiji

Acknowledgments

First, to my lovely typist, Hannah Singhurse, who has journeyed with me now for seven books! Her professional work has enhanced my manuscripts.

Next, to Candance Johnson of the Print Shop, who, likewise, has journeyed with me through seven books. Her professional work with me on book covers has allowed me to design my own covers to my liking.

Last, but not least, Linn Hartman, who has spent countless hours working with me to research the travels of Captain James Cook and Captain William Bligh, gathering facts to rewrite in story form for a good adventure!

This journey started on a Sunday afternoon. It began with a phone call again, and Captain Mobley was calling me to check on me and also to bring me up-to-date on the latest news. Funny thing, I was rolled back in my recliner, trying for a nap, but my mind had kicked into memories.

I remember the first time I met Captain Dick Mobley. This is a lengthy journey in itself, this meeting of my friend. It was by chance. I had decided to make one more return to Canada to relive old memories of the good times I had spent going to see friends for nine years. Good times fishing, hunting, and spending quality time in the north woods in an area called Mountain Ash Lake, a place where my friend spent several years as a fire spotter in a hundred-foot fire tower.

He and his wife had quarters in a rustic log cabin, which was located right next to the lake. Every two weeks, the forestry sent in a beaver, as they were called, a pontoon de Havilland airplane. It landed on the lake and taxied to the pier to unload supplies. Also during the time we were not in the north woods, our gathering place was at St. Joseph Island, Nelson's Campground, sites for travel, trailers, and also log cabins for rent.

I wanted to revisit all the old-time places I had been, maybe for the last time! But that was long ago, and now my thoughts moved ahead to my meeting of Captain Mobley. There his ship was, docked at the bay docks. It just about blew my mind to see that ship docked there. It was a three-masted sail ship and built like the HMS *Vanguard* that I was familiar with.

I couldn't help approaching this oddity and looking it over. Looking on the back, I saw the name, *Sheila*. Just then, the owner approached me and said, "Hello, James!"

I asked, "How do you know me?"

He said, "The dock keeper explained to me who you are." After a long chat, I was invited to come aboard, and next morning, to sail away with him. But that was long ago, and yes, I went, and it is all explained in *Odyssey Down Under*, book one. Each time, as in the story, it starts with Captain Mobley calling me from Australia, and another journey to another part of the world is in store.

As I started to say before I had to repeat a little background information, Captain Mobley was calling me again. This time, he did not have his usual jovial chuckle that was so typical of him. It was all seriousness as he started his conversation. It wasn't the happy, laughing friend that took me on our first journey of a lifetime!

I answered the phone. "Good afternoon, mate. It's afternoon here, so it must be early morning in Australia?"

"Yes, James, it is. I've wanted to call you but put it off for a spell! I wanted to get my thoughts in order before I did. I wanted to bring this situation into conclusion before we talked."

"What's wrong, Captain? You sound a little stressed?"

"Yes, mate, I am. I didn't know how you would take this situation."

"You worry me, mate. You sound serious, and that's not you, Captain Mobley!"

"Well, it's a long story, James. So I ask for your undivided attention. It is not all bad! Some good, but troubles on that you may feel betrayed as well as I did in the beginning! When I get the story told, you will see why, in the beginning, I felt a little betrayed. It involved Curt, my good friend. You remember he flew us over the Cook Islands on our cruise? There were so many to see, and there was no way we could approach them by sea. At the time, Curt was all excited, telling us about his partner from the service that joined in with him to fly freight, then later, they got another plane, and his friend refitted it to fly tourist. He told us all this when he flew down to the ship at Tasmania to take us on a tour by air, right?"

"Yes, go on, Captain."

"Well, Curt came to me now and gave the real story. He told a white lie, but he did not mean it in a bad way and asked my forgiveness. I was proud that he was man enough to do that! He was really trying to protect a friend. He wanted to be sure that everything was in place before he owned up!

"Now that it was confession time, and he came to me, he came to clear the air." Captain chuckled, so I knew he was starting to feel relief. "Now we know that Curt had to give a little story about his mate, but he really didn't have to bring it up at all. I guess he was trying to cover all bases.

"Now all this all started when Curt saw an ad on the Internet. The forestry in Canada were putting some de Havilland seaplanes on the market. They were good craft, but the forestry wanted to reduce some in order to buy some Huey helicopters that would enhance their operation. Make land and water more versatile. Curt bid on the best one offered, and he was surprised when he went on the bid. The forestry contacted Curt and said the plane was ready for pick up! Curt replied back and said he was not available to travel for pick up. Would they deliver for a fair price? They agreed and said they would recruit a pilot and notify Curt when he was en route.

"Later on, Curt was contacted, and the message was a flight plan. Aircraft has been released, will leave Ontario, Canada, fly to Corpus Christi, Texas, USA, refuel, resume flight to Tahiti, from Tahiti to Samoa. The message went on to say that the pilot would be carrying all necessary papers for customs, and all legal papers and history of the aircraft to deliver to Curt. Curt was to wire payment to Canadian forestry in Ontario, Canada. The pilot would be carrying airfare to fly back in return.

"There was a delay, but Curt did not get too concerned. If time rocked on, he would check that Curt then was notified to come to the airfield and receive his plane. When Curt got to the airfield and approached his now legally owned second plane, the pilot opened the door and climbed out. That's when Curt was shocked. Curt said he was a real live Indian. Not from India, but a real live Indian from a tribal family! Buckskins, moccasins, long black hair, braided, dark complexion, the whole deal.

4

"He shook hands with Curt and said, 'Hello, I'm Hawk!'

"After all legal formalities were complete, Curt said, 'Well, you don't have to go right back, so stay on a few days and see Samoa! You can bunk in with me. You need a rest after a long journey like that.'

"Hawk said, 'That's mighty kind of you, sir. I guess I could stay on a spell, long as it was within reason.'

"So now, James, you will meet Curt's *real* partner. After you hear the rest of it. It was not the first story we heard from Curt, but I call it justified because he was protecting a friend," said Captain.

"Continue, Captain!" I said.

"Okay. So Curt said to Hawk, 'You were a little over on the timing. Was there a problem?'

"Hawk said, 'No, I must confess to you, I took an illegal diversion. I flew off course to Fiji. I have an uncle living down there that I have not seen since I was a child.'

"Curt smiled and said, 'That's understandable, Hawk! That's family!'

"So Curt took Hawk under his wing and gave him the grand tour of the island. Hawk then moved Curt's new plane over to Curt's airfield. They talked planes, looked at planes, flew the plane, and the two of them had a great time. Hawk stayed on with Curt, and it was no time at all that a strong friendship spawned!

"A few days later, Curt asked how long could Hawk extend the visit.

"Hawk replied, 'If I stay longer, the Canadian government will be tracking me down!'

5

"'Why?' Curt asked.

"Hawk replied, 'When I go back, the government will force me back on the reservation!'

"Curt yelled, 'WHAT?'

"'Yes, I have to return. The forestry does not have the control over me, only when they can provide me employment, and that is sometimes short-lived, and back I go!'

"It's a long story. If you want me to tell, I will tell!" Captain said, then went on. "So, James, that is how he got his partner. Let me go on as how, and then I want to give you Hawk's history, as told to me by Curt!

"So Curt was so shocked by his story that he told Hawk he was not going back if he had anything to do with it. Curt took the whole story to the powers that be on consulate American Samoa. After much deliberation, Hawk was granted an American citizenship with legal papers, social security card, the whole nine yards! He didn't have to go back!

"Curt said, 'You are my partner now! Send your return ticket and papers copy back to Canada!'

"So, James, that is how Curt got his partner. Hawk is the one who did all the work on the plane revisions and update, also convinced Curt to drop freight and go into moving tourists. He revised the planes, founded an aircraft engine firm, traded their old engines for new turboprop, and all necessary revisions. The business has become very strong! Recently, they flew into Sydney after contacting me and stayed over for a day. Curt was so excited to show off Hawk!"

"Wow! Captain, that was some deal! I'm glad Hawk got his freedom!"

"Well, James, while I go you captive, I may as well bring you the rest of the story. Then I have facts written down about Hawk's history that I just have to share with you!"

Hawk's history

Hawk was born in Ontario, Canada. His mother was Ojibwe Indian, and his father was Scottish. The baby was born with the complete complexion of an Indian baby, with coal black hair and the bluest of blue eyes. The proud father wanted to name him "Hawkins McGregor," after the Scotch. The mother said, "No. My little Indian boy cannot grow up with the name of Hawkins! We shall call him Hawk! He shall be Hawk McGregor."

The father then said, "So be it!"

Hawk grew up as a strong boy. He was schooled in the best of schools in Ontario. When Hawk was nearing his teens, tragedy struck! His father, a hearty, robust, Scotchman, contracted a serious illness and did not survive it. His passing left wife and son to fare for themselves. They were heartbroken and struggling for a direction. Hawk's mother wanted to go back to her own people, the Ojibwe.

Contacting the government, she was allowed to take her son and assimilate back with the tribe. This put Hawk in a bad position. He was now a tribal member and had to conform with the laws governing the indigenous people.

Rather than fight the system, he applied himself to continue his education. He continued his studies and graduated from the Indian school. He applied for college, gained entry, and he was sharp in his studies. He earned a four-year degree in the field of aviation. Hawk loved airplanes and flying! More so than the studies, but he pushed on until he received his master's degree.

Hawk was so well-versed in the construction and application of aircrafts that his instructor said, "I believe Hawk could disassemble a complete aircraft, blindfolded, and correctly reassemble it to its original position!"

But Hawk still had the love of flying in his blood. He took flying school and earned his license. His instructor said, "Hawk is a natural. He first time he took off the ground, I knew he didn't need help training. He just needed the credentials."

Hawk then landed a job with the forestry. They needed a part-time pilot on call, whenever situations created a need for extra manpower. Hawk soon became valuable to the forestry with his knowledge and flying ability! He was top pilot! But the budget wouldn't allow it. The Canadian government recognized Hawk as a member of the Ojibwe tribe, so by law, he was to return to the reservation when not employed!

Hawk hated this. He petitioned against it on the basis that he was the son of a Scotch-Canadian citizen, emancipated, and should have his freedom! The government still said no! He was assimilated back into the tribe with his mother at a young age. The forestry went also on his behalf, and the government said no! So after each job assignment was complete and forestry had a lull, Hawk had to return to the reservation.

The new opportunity

Captain Mobley paused, then continued his story. "Well, James, that's Hawk's history, but fortunately, another event takes place that allows the forestry to call for his service again. The Canadian forestry wanted to purchase some helicopters to enhance their operations. They needed the capability of the chopper helicopter to master landing on any terrain where the de Havilland couldn't go.

"This dictated a reduction of several de Havilland seaplanes. To expedite this, the forestry put the aircraft on the market—purchase by bid on suggestion price, description of plane age, condition, service hours, etc.

"Our friend Curt, seeing the ad, placed a bid on the one he thought would be best. He said to me that it was an opportunity that was once-in-a-lifetime, and although he had a plane, he hated to pass it up. No big deal if he didn't get the bid!

"So later, to his surprise, he was notified by the Canadian forestry that he had top bid on the aircraft of his choice. They indicated that he should come with a certified check, and aircraft would be signed over to him with all legal documents. Curt said there was no way he would be available, and could they make the delivery? After some more negotiations, they agreed on a delivery price and would notify him when the aircraft left the ground in

Canada, its flight plan, and estimated date of delivery. The forestry thought that, to help him out, Hawk should make the delivery! So flight plan was made by the forestry. Leave Canada to Corpus Christi, Texas, refuel! Then southwest to Tahiti for a short layover, then on to American Samoa to buyer.

"Well, James," said Captain Mobley as he chuckled. "When he got to Tahiti, there was a little unscheduled detour! He flew on down to Fiji! Seems he had a relative down there which the family hadn't contacted for years. His name was Magnus McGregor, a brother to his father! Uncle Magnus, known to the population as 'Scottie.'

"Now get this, James! He was the old Scotchman that you and your wife saw swim to his boat every day, tied out on the post of the security fence! Seems as though he kept a modest apartment at the Radisson Hotel in Fiji!

"So after the visit, he took a direct flight to Samoa and Curt. When he arrived, he confessed to Curt about the detour and apologized. Curt liked the young man and asked him to stay on for a while and check him out on the de Havilland he had bought. Also to go over his own, since he had the knowledge.

"So a friendship was born between the two pilots! Hawk opened up more and more to his situation! When he went back, he would again be confined to the reservation, since the Canadian government had denied his rightful citizenship. Well, Curt was quite taken with all this and contacted some officials at the government to be in the American Samoa. Wheels were turned, and Curt got Hawk a permanent citizenship. Hawk sent a copy of the legal papers, along with the return flight tickets to the Canadian forestry and bid farewell!

"So, James, that's how Curt acquired his partner, not by the stories he first told us. He was protecting his friend!" Captain chuckled again and said, "Hold on, James. There's a little more to this!

"Seems like when Hawk knew he was to take this assignment, he slipped off and took an unscheduled trip to the Mountain Ask Lake area. There he met up with Eagle Feather, your old friend you spent time with there! Don't ask me how, but you know the Indians have ways that we don't know about!

"Eagle Feather was a respected elder of the Ojibwe tribe. Hawk wanted to confide in him before he left. He told Eagle Feather his assignment and asked what he should do because he didn't want to come back!

"Eagle Feather thought for a long time, then spoke to Hawk. 'I can tell you that I have lived for years in this north country and will 'til I die! The Canadian government has searched for years to put me on the Ojibwe reservation. But they have failed! Finally, they just gave up! What I did was illegal in their eyes but legal in mine! I cannot counsel you to do something that is illegal! I can only tell you to follow your heart, and let the great spirit set the path you must take.'

"Hawk agreed that he would take his advice. Then he said to Hawk, 'We must visit for a while longer, for I may never see you again. I wish to tell you a story about my friend, James, who came here one day. We became close friends and spent many happy hours together.

'He came here in a quest for a white wolf that he had contact with many years ago. An impossible dream. But James believed in the animal spirits and the great spirit! In time, his quest was fulfilled.'

"He was silent for a while, and then he spoke again. 'On this journey you are about to take, my son, you may run into James. I have this feeling that you will. If you do, please tell him that you and I talked. Also that I'm still in our beautiful north woods, and I travel with a white wolf!'

"So, James, what do you think about all that?"

"Wow! Captain, that is almost unbelievable!"

"Well, yes, it is unbelievable. I was glad that Curt brought the story to me. It relieved my mind that he was seeking forgiveness from what he had told us in the past. Yet, it was necessary to protect a friend. So he didn't mean it in a bad way.

"After he knew all the paperwork was legal and secure, he felt it was time to come to me." Captain started to chuckle, then he spoke. "James, remember our last cruise to the top of the world and then down to Hawaii?"

"Yes, I do, and I will never forget that trip!"

"Remember the crowds that gathered to the *Sheila II*, thinking we were a cruise line?" He chuckled. "Well, I didn't want to disappoint those folks, so I gave them Curt's phone number and told them he would fly them anywhere they wanted to go, cheaper and better!

"Well, the news went like wildfire. Curt got so many calls that he had to take Hawk and both planes to Hawaii. He and Hawk had to stay in Hawaii for a month, transporting tourists. They even made bookings for next year!" Captain laughed because he had pulled something off!

Then he went on to say, "Glad I did it, though. It sure enhanced their business."

"Captain, I really enjoyed all this news! It just makes my day! A really big day! Now I think there is more to the story!"

Captain started laughing again. "Yes, James. Are you ready for another trip?"

"Well, give me the details, Captain, because you know I will say yes!"

"Curt called me. He wants to come to Sydney and meet with me. I guess for confession and restitution!" Then he chuckled. "He wants to come with Hawk and introduce him to me. When he called, I was on the station. I would have to make arrangements to go to Sydney. I will call in the crew to Captain Cook's dock and have a field day. The boys and I will give the *Sheila* a good spring clean for next trip out. No trip now, though.

"Curt said, 'For one night, me and Hawk will bunk on plane.'

"'But crew will be gone then, so you can bunk on ship.'

"Curt and Hawk flew in from Samoa on the new plane that Curt had delegated to Hawk as a partner. During the visit, a plan was struck."

Captain went on, "Hawk wants to meet you since his visit with your friend, Eagle Feather! And he wants to take you, me, and Curt to return to Fiji to meet with Uncle Magnus! Curt says all expenses are paid. This is on their business expense account. Hawk is anxious to talk with you since his conversation with Eagle Feather. He said to tell you that Eagle Feather is still travelling the north country, and he has a white wolf that stays by his side!

"James, since you were last here, Hawk has also upgraded Curt's plane as well. They found an aircraft engine company and parts. They traded in the old engines and installed new turboprop engines with Hawk's know-how! Lighter, more power, and fit the same housing! Both planes are now fully restored. They can accept twelve passengers but prefer to keep the passengers at ten. Both planes, if needed, can carry up to twenty, plus pilot.

"Both planes took their maiden flight to the Hawaiian islands to serve the tourists. They have been on demand ever since the word spread. If it's a small crowd, Curt and Hawk both go. If large, they fly separate but on the same route."

"Captain, I am curious about something! How do the passengers take Hawk as an Indian in buckskin?"

"James, they love it! They fight to get on his plane if two are required to go! Hawk is a smooth pilot and also a smooth talker. He can lecture about the islands they are about to see or he can tell Indian stories. The passengers all want to hear the Indian stories! They can see the islands. He sometimes talks both and also recites poems from Hiawatha. They can't get enough!

"Like the major airlines, they carry little donation envelopes behind the seats. These are for passengers that don't want to bother with money exchange back. All currency is acceptable, state what charity you wish. Curt carries them, and Hawk also added to his donations of your choice or donations for the needy Ojibwe poor. His envelopes are always full. The ones for Ojibwe, he makes one check and mails to the tribal consul.

"I know that it is a lengthy answer, James, but I wanted to get it all in!"

Future plans

After all the good information was discussed, I asked Captain Mobley if I should make preparations to head that way!

He said, "May as well! I'm still here in Sydney with the crew. I'll call Curt and tell him to come on. It will be a short time for him to get prepared with Hawk, so that gives you ample time to get here. As soon as you arrive, the crew wants a short visit, then they will return home. Cookie will give us our last really good meal!

"Don't go to Menzies Hotel. Come on to the ship. Only you and I will be here for a night or two, waiting on the plane."

So I said, "Then I understand that the crew won't be involved in this flight?"

"Right, James. Just you, I, Curt, and Hawk. Hawk will fly us to Fiji for an uncle visit and a little sightseeing, then fly us back."

"So quick and clean, eh, Captain? No detours, no after cruise parties, and so forth?"

"Right, mate," and he chuckled. "This trip is our solo!"

"Sounds good. I'll start to plan to fly over, down under!"

"Oh, and one more thing, James, before we close off here. When you check in at LA for Qantas Air, Leilani will be there, holding your round-trip ticket!" Then he chuckled.

"Captain, what is going on?"

"Well, James, be a good sport about this, mate! Don't get angry! I took the liberty of buying your ticket, and then remembering you went first class, two seats. That's what it is. Now a guy doesn't need to sit in two seats alone, so I contacted Leilani." He chuckled. "She has some free flights coming from Qantas, so she will be on your flight coming and going." He chuckled again.

I started to say something, but Captain cute me off. "James, here is an opportunity for you and Leilani to be together coming and going! James, that young lady has a serious crush on you!"

"I know, Captain, but you know my position on flights. No doubt I enjoy the company, but I don't see us getting together."

"Well, give it a go, mate. You never know. Stranger things have happened! Well, mate, I'm signing off. Have a good trip."

It was a good trip at that, Leilani and I to Australia.

When we arrived, I took a cab from the airport straight to Captain Cook's dock. When I arrived, the whole crew was anxious to greet me and talk old times. Cookie was preparing supper but took time to chat. "I'll do supper tonight, James, and breakfast in the morning before they boys and I leave. All will be cleaned up, shipshape!"

"Thanks for that, Cookie! Looks like we will have to get in another trip to get together."

"Yes, I imagine we will!" We had that night together and breakfast in the morning, then the crew made their departure.

Our flyboys were due in later that day. Time went pretty quick for us, and then we heard the drone of an aircraft engine. Coming off the horizon, flying low, was the beautiful de Havilland. Teal blue, accented in white, and that engine purring like a kitten. The pilot circled the bay once before he brought his plane down. The plane came down smooth as silk, kissed the water, and smoothly headed for the dock! Nearing them, he reversed the engine and made a smooth approach to dockside.

The dockhands were on the ball and had an electric departure ramp heading for the plane door. Hawk and Curt secured the plane to the ramp. Curt came forward, and Hawk announced departure! I looked at Captain Mobley, and he looked at me with just as much surprise! People came pouring out of the plane, all excited and giddy— laughing, smiling. And Captain and I just stood there, looking dumb.

Hawk came on dock, shook our hand, and said, "Be right back!" He led the folks up the dock and turned them loose on the vendor. Curt never said a word. I guess he figured it was Hawk's story!

As Hawk came back, I noticed all the Aboriginal folks were completely astonished with Hawk. Who was this dark-skinned man, dressed in buckskin, and walking softly? Someone said they had never encountered him! Normally, the Aboriginals would not look straight at you or not in your eye! They believe if they looked a White man in the eye, he would steal their soul! But they had no problem looking at Hawk! This dark-skinned man with long, coal black hair and the bluest of eyes.

Hawk came back to us with a grin on his face, introduced himself, and shook hands all around. He spoke! "I know you folks are confused," he said with a grin. "So let me explain. Before we left Samoa, these folks came looking for a charter service to Fiji. Well, I was going to Fiji! So I said, 'Look, folks, I can take you to Fiji, but I have to pick up two passengers in Sydney to go to Fiji. I know that is a little out of the way. If you are dissatisfied, I'll return your money. But if you want to fly with me, I'll make a deal! No charge for flight to Sydney, and then your normal fee to Fiji.

"'We will have one-night layover, and I can book you into the Menzies Hotel on a discount! Also, a free breakfast! And then today they will have their courtesy bus take you all on a short tour of the city. Then this evening, the bus will take you to the world-famed Opera House for a free performance. Then back to Menzies Hotel. In the morning, they will bring you back to Captain Cook's dock to board the flight to Fiji! Now who wants their money back to recharter?'

"'No! No! No!' was the cry. They wanted to fly with this Indian and get all the freebies on a side trip!" Then he laughed! "We will have them going to Fiji, but once there, at the end of their stay, they will book a Qantas flight non-stop to the States!"

Captain Mobley started laughing and said, "I think I am going to love this guy!"

We then went back together to the *Sheila II*, and Captain Mobley took us all on a tour of the ship! I knew the ship by heart since all our journeys together, but I wanted to hear Captain Mobley's narration.

That evening before turning in for the night, Hawk wanted to hear all about my trip to Canada in search of the white wolf and my meeting with Eagle Feather and our time spent together. They all listened spellbound at my long story. Hawk was duly impressed. That was his favorite elder of the Ojibwe tribe. I told Hawk, whenever he got back to the wilds of Canada, to look up Eagle Feather and tell him about our chat and where.

Hawk said, "I sure will do that! I need to go back from time to time to visit my mother. I know how to contact Eagle Feather in the Mountain Ash area." I didn't respond. A little silence, then Hawk said, "I can go back now as an American citizen, thanks to Curt!"

Chapter 7

Bright and early the next morning, we were up! With Captain Mobley, I guarantee you will be up early! We secured all and went back down to the plane. It wasn't long before Hawk's little group of ten came down the pier, laughter and chatter filling the air. The dockhands were right out there, and the folks boarded and went to their assigned seats. That left two behind Curt and Hawk, reserved for the captain and me!

Hawk untied, and the gangway was withdrawn. The plane door was closed and checked to be secure, and our pilot, Hawk, took his seat. The engine rumbled into life, and we sat a minute to let it warm up. Then Captain Hawk, who was in control now, put the engine in reverse, slowly backing out into the bay. He turned the plane to head out and hesitated while he called air control to give his code number and ask clearance for takeoff. He stated his destination and asked for all clear. No jetliners descending anywhere near his path of travel. All clear!

Easy throttle forward, and the de Havilland was scooting smooth across the water—lift off—gained proper altitude! Then Hawk spoke in his mic, "Fiji bound, folks!"

And a big cheer went up! "Everybody happy?" said Hawk. A big cheer again.

When we made proper altitude, Hawk asked, "Okay, folks, what do you want to hear? Stories about Fiji or Indian stories?"

They all yelled like kids at a ball game. "We want Indian stories!"

Captain and I looked at each other and grinned! Everyone settled in for the flight. It wouldn't be a long one. It was a good day to fly!

We started to fly over small islands of Fiji, and I did not realize there were so many. Years ago, when we flew in, it was at night—dark—and when we flew in the airport, we really didn't know where we were. Taking a taxi across the main island, it was breaking dawn, so we could see the countryside and see how the Fijians lived. It looked like a poor life, and we saw a man plowing his field with an old-style, primitive wooden plow hooked to an ox. When we got to the Radisson Hotel, it was a completely different world.

When I came here with Captain Mobley, years later, I learned how advanced the islands were with modern ways of life, plantations, high tech industry, state-of-the-art colleges, and a big advancement in government. The Indian population that once had been indentured servants to the Fijians were now all intermarried with Fijians and several other nationalities and were prospering and highly educated. It was now the land of the people, not just the Fijians.

Soon, we approached the big island of Viti Levu. Hawk said we would land at Suva, the largest airport in the islands. This was where most of the major flights came in and went out. Hawk reported in and got clearance for a runway. One of the passengers got a little anxious and said, "There's no water!"

Hawk chuckled and said, "We got wheels!"

Then the landing wheels were lowered out of the pontoons, and the gentleman was relieved. He let out a "Whew." Hawk taxied up to the tarmac, and a motorized stairway was coming alongside. Hawk and Curt went out first to bottom of stairway. Captain Mobley and I went next when we saw that Hawk and Curt were in position to greet the passengers and welcome them to Fiji!

At this airport, you walked the tarmac to an entrance of the main building. Everybody was excited, and passengers were hugging Hawk and Curt, thanking them for an extraordinary adventure! A lot of smiles, hugs, and "Thank yous," and the group headed in the terminal.

Captain Mobley asked, "When do we come back to pick them up?"

Hawk said, "We don't. They will book a direct flight back to the States. Now we are not staying here. We will get clearance, and then fly across the island to the shopping center dock facilities that Captain Mobley uses on his pass bys. The shuttle bus still runs on the hour, back and forth to the Radisson and other beach hotels! Reservations for us are made at the Radisson.

"I also learned that Uncle Magnus has a yearly agreement at one of the separate apartments at the Radisson.

That's where I stayed when I did a sneak away—on the off-course flight to Samoa." Then he looked at Curt and grinned. Curt never responded. He just smiled. He didn't care! He found a friend and partner!

After customs were returned to the plane, Hawk contacted the tower and asked for clearance and a runway. As we lifted off, Hawk started chuckling. "We got wheels!" A short flight, and we were landing at the shopping center on water. Hawk brought his aircraft in so slick you could hardly feel the pontoons touch the water. We taxied in, secured the plane, checked in with security, and before you knew it, we were on the shuttle bus to Radisson on the beach!

Meeting Uncle Magnus

We checked in and were guided to our rooms. Walking through the lobby, I noticed it was roofed over by open-air. The bar was also open-air. The interior garden was beautiful with all native trees and flowers, walk paths, a pool with waterfalls, and a stone's throw from the beach.

I looked down a ways to the property line, and there was Magnus, boat softly moving up and down, tied to the corner of the protected beach fence a way out. On to our rooms, and we had two adjoining rooms, outside balcony, two queen beds each room. Wall-in showers and a fridge with all kinds of goodies, stocked every day, microwave, coffee pot. What more could you ask for?

Hawk said, "We have the biggest part of the day left. What say we enjoy ourselves and check on Uncle Magnus late this afternoon?" We all agreed, and before you can blink an eye, Hawk was digging in his pack and came out with a pair of shorts, stripping down into the shorts, and yelling, "Last one in the pool is an Indian!"

He laughed and took off running. We all hustled into our shorts and were not far behind. I was last in, so I was the Indian. They were all laughing, and I said, "I don't mind being an Indian. In fact, I feel rather proud."

Captain Mobley was laughing and said, "James, you are a crazy bloke!" It was good to be around close friends.

Later, we went over to Magnus's penthouse, so he called it. He had rented it and told the manager, "You just keep renewing this for me, year by year until I'm gone." Magnus, we soon learned, was full of surprises.

We knocked, and this Scotchman opened the door. A stout little man with a perpetual smile, fair complected and reddish hair mixed with gray, and the bluest eyes. When he saw Hawk standing and grinning at him, his eyes became misty, and he grabbed Hawk in a bear hug. "So nice to see you again, son!"

Then Hawk made introductions. When Magnus shook my hand, he said, "For some reason, I know you, or have I seen you?"

"Yes, Magnus, you did, but we didn't connect then. Years ago, when I visited Fiji for the first time, I used to watch you sitting on the beach, same time every day! Then you would walk into the water and wade out. Then have to swim to the corner of the protective fence, duck under hole, climb on your boat, and away you went! Next day, same routine!'

Magnus laughed. "I still do that, mate, every day. Sometimes I'm lucky to have a paying customer to take over to some island! When we get settled, I'll show you the map. Come in, come in!"

Magnus couldn't wait to pull out his map of Fiji and surrounding islands, different sizes, and different locations. The map showed that, besides the two major islands, there were fifty smaller ones scattered about. Magnus said he may have missed a few. The two major islands plus the smaller ones were all undermined by a reef. One that varied in depth, so a ship would have travel in care. It made me think of Captain Cook on the *Endeavor*, investigating these islands!

Magnus said he thought he must have touched all of them through the course of the years. Then he paused to say, "I'll take you boys on a little tour in the next days!" Then on to say, "Most of the islands are accessible by boat and a lot by air, if they have room for a landing strip. Most cannot take a large jetliner, but small aircraft would have no problem."

Then he held the map up and with a chuckle, he asked, "Okay, guys, which ones do you want to see?" We just looked at each other and rolled our eyes! "Just teasing, mates. I'll take you to some with most interest. You know, some are inhabited! Some natives live in the old way, but they don't eat people." He laughed heartily.

"In past history, that was true, but long past. Some folks make their home there but travel every day or so, many days a week, to hold a job on the main islands, Viti Levu and Vanua Levu. Most are Fiji natives, Indian, or mixed! They take on all the manual tasks. When you meet one, they will say, 'Bula.' Sounds like 'boola.' That's their greeting. Then when they take a liking to you, it's 'Bula bula'!" And he chuckled.

"I guarantee you mates an exciting adventure! Now let's hear some of your stories. I know there must be many out of you four! I'm so very happy to have my long-lost nephew again. I miss my brother, but I am glad that my sister-in-law is doing well back in the Ojibwe tribe. I am thrilled to have Hawk for a short time, and I sure am happy to meet you men! Gets a little lonely sometimes in my solitary life! Now let me take you down to the restaurant on the beach for an evening meal! Then let's tell stories, and you guys can bunk in with me. Will talk about tomorrow's plans."

Hawk spoke up. "We have rented rooms, Uncle, but we will make plans tonight for tomorrow. But I for one will not be swimming outside the protection fence for the boat!"

Magnus roared with laughter. "I won't put you through that. You boys can take the shuttle bus to the shopping center, and old Magnus will be waiting there on my boat!"

So Magnus wasn't ready to call it a night. He looked at us all and said, "Let's go down to the restaurant on the beach and see if we can find something good. The treat's on me. Then let's come back home for a spell and tell stories about each of you." He laughed.

26

"I'm not ready to give up on my nephew right away. It has been many years past. I need to get caught up on my brother and his wife. Also Hawk's growing up. Let's hear of some Indian stories which he tells on his flights, and you, Curt, you are the copilot on some of his runs, and you can relate.

"Now, Captain Mobley, I know you and James have a lot to tell about your meeting and adventures together!"

Captain Mobley chuckled. "We will have to spread the stories out during our stay. I'd keep you up all night if I tried to tell all!"

Magnus looked at me. "James, how about you?"

"Well, Magnus, I will be in most of Captain's stories since he has made me a south seas traveler! But yes, I may bring some tall tales that none of you have heard!"

Old Magnus laughed again. "I may have some tall tales about my travels around all these small islands!"

So dinner on the beach, and then we sat to a late hour with stories to entertain Magnus as well as ourselves!

The shopping center excursion

To say you were going to the shopping center to catch a boat would perplex some folks, but actually, that was where the docking facilities were. We arrived in the shuttle bus in the morning, and as we walked down the shopping center courtyard, we could see Magnus's boat, gently rising and falling in the waters of the dock. He arose to greet us, trying not to disclose the fact that he had been asleep.

Shaking hands and giving Hawk a big hug, he said, "Welcome to my boat! Not like Captain Mobley's *Sheila II*, but it serves me well! Come aboard and let me tell you about the ole girl here! First of all, folks, it is an old Chris-Craft that has been totally restored. It has two Chrysler marine engines that supply more power than you need! Slopping stern that allows easy access out of the water on to the back deck. The cab over can be fully closed off if need be.

"Sleeping quarters are four bunks, and I carry some nice sleeping bags for those who wish to sleep on deck. A small galley with stove, refrigerator, sink, and also a little freezer, toilet facilities forward in the bow, small shower, sink, and stool, ample cabinets around, and storage under the bunks and also under the bench seats on deck!

"This boat has been my life for years, and it's like part of me! I keep it up-to-date, and I have a Fijian man who is a qualified mechanic go over it frequently. This boat came from the US. James, have you ever seen one?"

"Yes, as a boy, I went to a boat show that was specializing in different boat models of the Chris-Craft. I always dreamed of one day having one. I guess that's one of the factors that drew me into the navy. Instead of a big ship, I would have rather been assigned to a patrol craft, but it didn't turn out that way."

"Okay!" Magnus spoke. "Are we ready to get underway?"

"Yes, we are ready and also anxious."

Magnus looked at us with a grin. "I don't know how long you boys want to make a go of it, but we will keep going until you say 'uncle.'" And he laughed. He idled out off the small bay there, and then when he hit coastal waters, he hit the throttle! The two-marine engines kicked in, and we were flying across the top of the water, smooth as silk! Almost like one of those hydroplanes.

Magnus was the guide. We had no particular request. This was his excursion to entertain his friends! We headed south from the Pacific Harbor, past a near island, Beqa, had a sightseeing run around that small island, then headed southwest to Vatulele, which supported an airport. Magnus said it was one of the islands they could fly you in for a beach stay!

Then on south to the Kadavu Passage, which supported islands, Tauki and Kadavu. I should remark that most of all the Fiji Islands, great and small, were established centuries ago on a reef!

After touring this group, Magnus headed straight east to a little island of Matuku. Marinas and airports are frequent on most islands. I say most because some islands might accommodate small aircrafts like Hawk's, but other islands may only have a marina. This island we were approaching was extremely southwest of the main islands and looked like nowhere! Magnus found the marina and docked. He said his friend Fuji lived there and catered to travelers.

As we walked in off the pier, we saw several spread-out structures made of poles, round and thatched grass or reed roof covers made like a cone. The sides were all open and had covers to drop down in case of foul weather.

Fuji ran and grabbed Magnus's hand, yelling, "Scottie, Scottie, my friend. Welcome to my island!" Fuji was

Filipino and Fijian mix. That is a nice way to say it, but you understand it was intermarrying, which has been very prevalent in the islands. Magnus introduced us all around to Fuji, and he was all smiles.

"You must stay, Magnus. And your friends! I have a veranda open and a fresh pork coming off the spit. Other guests are here on vacation! I will serve you your supper at the veranda picnic table, and I want to hear your stories!"

Magnus turned to us. "Well, boys, looks like a night's stay." And he chuckled. We were happy. Short trip but ready to get off the water.

Fuji (pronounced "Foogee") soon had a campfire going near our picnic table. He had cooked for other guests, his family, and other friends on the island, so there was ample food to serve and even leftovers. Supper consisted of fresh pineapple, spit-roasted pork, a salad, and vegetables that I couldn't identify but very good. A native juice that looked like it could pack a punch, so I asked for water!

After supper, we thanked Fuji for the gracious accommodations. Curt said, "Fuji, that was the best pineapple that I have ever eaten!"

Fuji said, "You like? That came from Perry Mason's Island. He has big plantation there!"

Hawk looked in puzzlement at his uncle and said, "Who is Perry Mason?"

Magnus grinned and said, "That's Raymond Burr. He owns an island in Fiji and has developed a large plantation with various fruits. Also it is known that Mel Gibson owns an island here. I don't know what he does."

I spoke, "Yeah, I can testify to that! My first trip to Fiji, I had a man next to me that was from here who slept on my shoulder all night! Not by choice, though! My wife was better looking!" And Fuji got to laughing so hard he about fell off the bench!

So the stories started! And well into the night! When we went to bed, we were given a woven mat, some sort of pillow made, and a light cover. Looking up at the thatched cone of the roof, I thought, *This is not half bad!* The mat felt pretty good.

In the morning, Fuji insisted that he serve a good breakfast before we got underway. He had chickens, so it was fresh eggs, side of pork, and pancakes. I don't know what the pancakes were. Might have been poi, but they went down good! When we left, Fuji shook hands, and, misty-eyed, he said, "You friends come back and see Fuji!"

We hit the water, and Magnus said we would be heading to the Southern Lau Group.

After leaving Matuku, which is considered in the Koro Sea, which seemed so extremely south of the main island Vanua Levu, I felt I was out in nowhere. So far isolated and alone. So Magnus set course for the southern group of islands that are called the Southern Lau Group. Slightly to the north was a twin island named Totoya and Tivua. I know all these names in Fiji can be confusing, but I like to name them so our location can be monitored.

Magnus said, "Since just leaving an overnight stay, we will not be stopping on these two. They are pretty commercial now and gone modern. Large airport to fly in tourists. In my lifetime, I have at least visited every one of the fifty islands around Fiji. Mostly because my travelers did not have regular means of travel to get to some of them." Then he grinned and chuckled.

"Sometimes ole Magnus was a quicker mode of travel to get to some of these islands. Of course, that put money in ole Magnus's pocket!" Then he laughed, and we all laughed with him. Captain Mobley just roared with laughter, knowing sometimes a boat or ship was the best way!

Magnus went on to say, "My goal is to take you boys to the most picturesque island that I have visited and give you a view of something that has stood still in time and has not entirely advanced into the modern world. Some of these Fijian folks still want to live close to the old way, even though a little hardship is prevalent.

"We will move on to Kabara. There is a very small island above it that is totally uninhabited, something stuck in the past. That shows you somewhat what these islands looked like when discovered by Captain Cook." That stirred my mind, and later, I will have to express my thoughts about all this! When James gets quiet time! Right now, I don't want to miss a thing!

Magnus continued his narration, and there was not a comment for noise out of the group. Magnus was a good travel guide, and his story kept us spellbound. He went on. "We will be heading south and east to Fulaga, then on to Ogea Levu. This is the most southern island in the southern group. After an overnight stop, we will head north up into the northern group of islands. Incidentally, we are travelling in the Koro Sea, if none of you ever been here before!"

Captain Mobley raised his hand but did not speak! Didn't want to break the train of thought here!

Magnus went on, "I have friends here, so as guests, they will insist to feed us a good meal. No charge! But a little tip will be nice to help them out. It is against the law to tip in Fiji! I guess I do it anyhow because of the low income or no income of the people! We won't take a mat to sleep on tonight. We will stay on the boat. There is five people here, and I have four bunks. So do you want to draw straws?" And he laughed.

I spoke up. "No, Magnus. I will borrow one of your sleeping bags and sleep on deck! I have done that before!"

Magnus spoke. "Problem solved! Thanks, James."

When we arrived at the island, our docking facilities was a wharf house made with timber uprights and cut planks, all cut and lashed together with ropes made of material from the island. It wasn't pretty, but it was very sturdy! The natives kept their canoes tied there and also threw ropes off the wharf to net fish.

When we pulled in, the natives met us as we were tying up with cheers, smiles, and handshakes. Ole Magnus was back for a visit. After so much talk, Magnus took us on a hike up the hillside. Going up, we met a native coming down. Typical Fijian. Tall, muscular, a big grin on his face. He had a large yoke across his shoulders, a large container on each side. He continued on.

Magnus said, "There's a water source up here, and he is carrying down a supply of water." When we got to the top, Magnus showed to us a large pond of water. Off a cliff, a beautiful waterfall was tumbling down the rock into the pool. He then took us on a climb farther up where another clear pool was feeding the waterfall.

He then explained to us. There was a perpetual spring bubbling on into the top pool from deep within the volcanic rock. It continually keeps the top pool filled and spills into the waterfall and down to the bottom pool, which is kept full. This is their water source and has been flowing for eons!

We hiked down the hillside and took a tour of the village. Basic, primitive. Cooked over fires. The chief shook hands all around, and in perfect English said, "Magnus, you and your friends must stay the night and join us in a meal! We have been successful with the nets today and caught some splendid fish! Some mahi-mahi and a couple of barramundis, a very special fish to the islands and even Australians! We share that with you!"

So like Magnus said, dinner was ordered up! It consisted of cooked fish, some kind of root that tasted like sweet potato, and an herbal salad of some sort! All good, in fact, very delicious! We sat in a circle on the ground while we were served. Fresh water to drink or coconut juice of some kind. Maybe fermented! I chose water.

Sitting around the fire then, the stories began! Stories of the people and stories about Magnus and his friends. The visit went late into the night 'til all was said. Then everyone was off to bed. We were offered mats but chose to sleep aboard the boat.

Everyone settled in. I curled up on deck with my sleeping bag. The water was softly lapping against the hull of the boat. My mind started going back into the past. I couldn't shut down.

First I thought about all the island people in the fifty surrounding islands, as well as on the mainland. Most everything in the past had to be imported into Fiji. How did the people sustain on these small islands? The main islands had finally come to the forefront with modern technology. Main islands boasted state-of-the-art technology as well as medical and college expertise. Many countries or islands were traveling to Fiji for education, technology, produced goods, etc.

Then my mind went back to the beginning of time, so to speak, the time when the first Fiji travelers came and discovered these islands, back in ancient times! Historians have never figured out where they came from in their great sail canoes, but they came! What they found was a habitat that they wanted to take over and live on. So they came!

In the early days, there were many tribes. Each had a leader, and each had their own territory. But each desired what the other group had. So there were wars among them and takeovers and annihilation. IT IS RECORDED THAT THE FIJIANS were cannibals. They killed, then ate their enemies, even ate among their own tribe.

Then Captain James Cook came on the scene. He was surveying all the islands in the Pacific and claiming most for England. He saw promise in Fiji for an English possession. How he got all this information back to England in those long-ago days still baffles my mind! But that is another story in itself!

After Captain Cook got word to England, they sent in missionaries. These folks were successful in converting the native population. Teaching that war and cannibalism was wrong. England then sent in a governor to rule the realm. Fijians were taught vocations and how to farm.

The governor soon realized that the work was becoming overwhelming to the Fiji population, and he obtained indentured servants from India to be workers for the Fijians. When they served their time, they could become citizens, but they couldn't own land!

As time evolved, and Fiji advanced in knowledge and technology, the Indians intermarried. In time, the government made a decision to call them one people, and the ban was lifted. Now all Fiji citizens could own land, all could reap the benefits of education and move forward. This is something to think about. From cannibal to professional experts. I don't know how many people can own an island, but I'm told that Raymond Burr and Mel Gibson are two.

As I listened to the water slap against the side, I thought to myself, *I have to shut my mind down and go to sleep! I can't be sleeping in when my friends arise! Never live it down!*

Well, saved by the chief! Early in the morning, he was on the pier, yelling, "Arise, Magnus! We will have breakfast for you and your friends before you leave!"

We all awoke with sleepy eyes, so no one was caught. We got around and went ashore. The natives had side pork, eggs, and some kind of fire-baked bread prepared for us. After a good feed, we bid our new friends goodbye and thanked them for their hospitality!

North on the Koro Sea

There were still some islands in the north direction that we still classified as the southern group before we would enter into what was called the northern group. We moved up past Namaka Laua, which was a long island, narrow and small, and smaller than the length of its name. The next two up, Moce and Oneata, were so small, like dots on a page. We passed by for a scenic look and moved on.

Magnus said we would bypass a couple that would not present too much of interest and set course for Cicia, where we would refuel. That was putting us into the bottom of the Lau group. This island supported a major airport. Major airports meant major population and major hotels, etc. So our goal was to stick to the smaller islands, which were more to our liking and not so far advanced.

After refueling and a look around, we were off again! I was beginning to wonder about this old Scotchman. He plied these waters like a cruise ship. In a small boat, mind you! Not a thought in his mind as he crossed the Koro Sea! This was all in a day's journey for him. He has spent half a lifetime running from island to island as well as points on the two major islands. He knows them all, knows where to avoid the reef and where not!

His nephew, Hawk, was as alert as his uncle. He had no problem pronouncing the island names. I lend that to his upbringing in the Ojibwe tribe and mastering that language. Hawk also asked his uncle Magnus about history of the islands then and now.

This was opening up a new program for his flights with his seaplane. It would have no problem with reefs as it came in on top of the water. He could taxi right to the beach, and passengers with a yearning for a primitive vacation could book into one of the many scattered thatched cone-roofed shelters on a secluded beach, have a catered stay, and walk on the beach as a solitary visitor, enjoy the island foliage, no noise, no people, all to themselves. I think I could take a little of that myself.

Moving on north, we were approaching near the top of the northern chain—a long, narrow island, Vanua Balavu, which boasted two airstrips for a small island. It held good population and some commercialism. We had a quick look around and were satisfied.

From there we went due west to a tiny island no bigger than a speck on the map! Magnus suggested a rest stop there. When we pulled into the landing, a bunch of children came running! "Uncle Magnus!" they yelled—and Magnus had some treats stored for them—all dark, big eyes, and smiling faces.

An elder emerged from the little crowd. "Hello, Magnus. Welcome again! I hope for a little stay?"

Magnus grinned and said, "I hope for a few mats for an evening's sleep?"

"Will do, my friend, and your friends also. We will give you a meal tonight and a breakfast in the morning."

It was fish and rice. Very good. A night on mats in a thatched veranda! That was after a campfire and story session. Eggs and side pork in the morning. We were well-impressed with more of Magnus's friends. It was apparent that he treated them well in the past!

Morning brought an early rise and breakfast, as I said. All our goodbyes were said, and the children all gathered around to see this dark-skinned man with the long black braid of hair enter the boat! Their eyes big as silver dollars. Hawk got into Magnus's goody box and came out with a handful of candy. He threw it, with a big smile, to the kids, who, with big grins, scampered to gather it up!

When we got underway, Magnus called his nephew forward, saying, "I want you to take the wheel. Keep your course north–northwest. I want you to be able to say you navigated the Koro Sea!

"Folks, I want to take you across and show you the big peninsula that juts off the east side of the north island, Vanua Levu. No need to go on because it is very busy! It has four airports, and the highway off the mainland runs clear out to the tip of the connected islands. It is similar to the one you encountered in the north, Captain Mobley, when you visited the Aleutians and Alaska!" Captain Mobley acknowledged.

When we approached landfall, Magnus took the wheel back and gave his nephew a big pat on the back. "Right on the money, son! Thank you!" Magnus took us a for a joy ride up and down both sides of the connected land, along with a scattering of small islands around!

Now heading south again, we headed for an island in the middle of the Koro Sea, which is also named Koro. I imagine named after the sea itself. Koro had one airport on the southern side. Magnus said, "I know it's early, but tomorrow is a long run from Koro to the western side of the main island, Viti Levu. The northside of Koro is not as heavy with population, but there are good accommodations. We will rest there and fuel up.

"Tomorrow is a long run from Koro to the west side of the main island to the Yasawa group, where I want to take you boys next after Bligh Water. We will omit the islands just below us. They became heavily populated and are subject to custom stations. We are close to Koro Island, a good place to stop, refuel, and spend the night."

Koro was a beautiful island also centered east, about midpoint of all these islands, and east of Bligh Water and the two major islands. We were pleasantly surprised with accommodations the islanders here catered to fly-in tourists. Thatched-roof verandas were placed with ample distance from each other to provide guests with private time, quiet, and leisurely living. Native servants attended needs. A roofed-over, open-sided restaurant was located in ample distance. After having a good meal, we retired to our own little hut. Typical as others, you had a mat, a cover, and a small pillow!

We had just sat down, maybe ready for story time, when there was activity on the beach. The owners started a big bonfire for the enjoyment of the guests. The sun was slipping down on the horizon, its rays making a beautiful multicolor in the sky and on the water.

Then another activity started. A group of native men started dressing in their ancient ceremonial costumes. It was time for the lamp-lighting ceremony that was practiced over all these islands. It was an ancient ceremony of lighting the lights.

Every Fijian was a big man! Six-foot or over, like the ancient people. They lit torches and started trotting down the beach. At each veranda, there was a standing post with a large ball of combustible material. As they ran, they chanted and lit each post as they went clear to the end. The lamps were there to burn for the night, then refueled the next day for the next lighting of the lights.

Bligh Water

We sat quietly for a long time. Magnus broke the silence. "Well, boys, in the morning, we are heading for Bligh Water."

Captain Mobley asked, "Magnus, what is Bligh Water?"

Magnus in turn said, "It is the water between and around the islands, located between the two major islands. But in reality, extends clear to Tonga. It was named to commemorate the 'Mutiny on the Bounty', which occurred, and Captain Bligh and members were put adrift of the ship in a long boat."

"Is there more to the story, Magnus?" asked Captain Mobley.

"Well, yes, a whole lot more can be found, but ole Magnus never got into that. Most folks just take it for what it is."

Captain sat in silence for a while, and I know he was itching to know. He asked Curt and Hawk if they picked up anything in their travels?

"No," was their answer to that. I said nothing.

Then Captain Mobley looked at me! "I bet ole James here has something hidden away in his log about all this. Do you, James?"

I was trapped! "Well, yes, Captain, I do, but it is a very long story, and I mean, very long! It might take all night!" I said nothing more.

Hawk spoke up. "James, I want to hear that story! That would be good to know when I fly tourists down here!"

I looked at Hawk. "It might be longer than your flight!" Everybody laughed.

Ole Magnus nodded. "That lamp out there is going to burn all night! Ole Magnus wants to hear some history. I've lived here many years, and I just took it matter of fact. Like a good movie or a documentary. Like Hawk, I need to be educated. I boat people all over these islands, and I never know nothing. Only customs and such that I picked up from people. Heck! Go with it, boy! IF it takes all night, we will take another day and night here. Nobody is in a rush!"

Curt, the quiet one, raised his hand. "I guess I make it unanimous! The history holds too many interesting stories!"

"Well, okay!" I said. "Ole James will lay it on you, but I'm not kidding about an all-nighter. Captain Mobley, do you remember the story I told you about my friend, Linn? His cruise on the *Endeavor*?"

Captain chuckled. "Yeah, I remember the ole bloke who climbed the riggin'!"

"Well, he learned more than climbing the riggin'!" I paused. "When we had chats from time to time, he became a wealth of information, information that a lot of folks would like to know!"

Hawk said, "Well, James. Give it a go!"

I chuckled at that. "Hawk, Australia is rubbing off on you! You are already starting to talk like an Aussie!' Captain Mobley roared with laughter! "Well, Hawk, in order for ole James to give it a go, I warn you, it's a big go! To put things in proper perspective, we can't start with the mutiny. We need to stary with Bligh and Cook's assignments and what caused all this ruckus!

"We need to give Bligh proper recognition. To the public, he was a poor bloke who got into harm's way. But there is more to that. He and Captain Cook came up through the ranks tighter, seamen, advancing in rank! Each were dealt with assignments from the admiralty and even financed and blessed by ole King George! Each had long, hard journeys and assignments, or shall we say, they were dispatched!

"To tell the whole story, I need to wrap in Fiji, world conditions. America was having a war! This shut down the cotton enterprise, and England was needing cotton plus other goods. Hey! The whole world out there needed cotton and other commodities America supplied!

"So cotton barons started looking for places to set up and grow cotton around the globe. Their sights landed on many places—the Caribbean, South Sea islands, Fiji in particular. To grow cotton, you need land, then you need workers, so slave trade went rampant. Then you had to free the slaves.

"Food was running short with more and more slaves. The southern plantations in the Caribbean were increasing. Joseph Banks, a botanist, was on a cruise with Captain Cook. In Fiji he had found a plant that was a Fiji staple that they grew. It was called breadfruit and had a high nutritional value.

"When he returned to England, he built a relationship with merchants around the world. This breadfruit became a demand! The sugar plantations in the Caribbean required slave labor, and slaves required food. Everyone scrambling to obtain it. Breadfruit was the answer to many countries using slaves.

"The HMS *Bounty* was a large ship assigned to Captain Bligh. The plan was made to retrofit the *Bounty* to carry a large cargo, breadfruit in mind. So the voyages of the *Bounty* were designated to the south, specifically to Fiji. Mission to take breadfruit to the plantations in the Caribbean, and also to bring some plants back to place in the king's royal garden.

"The ship's main cabin was removed and other modifications to allow transport of breadfruit. The cargo held full, and as many as one thousand potted breadfruit plants on deck. Literally a floating greenhouse. Conditions on the ship became very cramped. Not only a full crew but also botanist, scientist, caregivers for plants were all cramped on board.

"One departure from England occurred in December 1789. Destination Tahiti. The journey required the bounty to cross the Atlantic Ocean, down around the cape of South America, and up to South Pacific destinations. Same in reverse. To travel to England, the second voyage, the *Bounty*, was stopped by big, severe winds, and the ship had to divert across the Atlantic Ocean to the continent of Africa, down around the horn into the Indian Ocean, then up the route to the South Pacific.

"Conditions between Bligh and his crew were becoming very strained. When they got to Fiji, the breadfruit crop was five months to harvest. So in the meantime, the crew took the opportunity to find girlfriends and other activities to their liking. When the time came for loading and departure, the crew became disgruntled and didn't want to go back to dreary and cold England.

"Ship loaded and one thousand plants on deck, the journey required a stop at Tahiti and on to Tonga. When they arrived at Tonga, conditions between Bligh and crew were beginning to come to a head. Forty miles from Tonga, Fletcher Christian leads a minority, and Bligh and loyalists are set adrift with the ship's longboat, twenty-three-foot-long, nineteen in the boat. Six loyalists had to stay aboard. No room in the boat! The mutineers left with the *Bounty*, and Bligh set sail for a nearby island.

"When they landed, immediately, one of the crew members was killed by a native. Bligh decided to set sail for Timor, which is approximately less than four thousand miles away to Jakarta. He instructed the crew, 'Only one ounce of bread and one-fourth pint of water per day!' He didn't want to head to Fiji for fear of cannibals. The crew was able to island hop and supplement their food supply. They went around the northside of Australia, and some folks questioned, 'Why?' What fear lay there?

"June of 1789, they arrived at Timor. Two months later, they arrived at Jakarta and waited for a ship departing for Europe. William Bligh, captain of the *Bounty*, finally makes it back to England and states his case!

"So, my friends, when we hit the Bligh Water tomorrow or whenever, remember the mutiny did not occur there. It was forty miles from Tonga. That is why they say the Bligh Waters extend to Tonga. But remember, Captain Bligh did plow the Bligh Waters here with his journeys to procure breadfruit." I don't know how long I was talking!

I looked around at the faces who looked at me. In amazement, Magnus, who was writing frantically, rested his pen. I said, "Anyone wanting a copy of this log, contact Magnus!" The group roared with laughter, even Magnus!

Then they asked, "What about Fletcher Christian and his band of mutineers?"

"That will indeed be another long part of the story. I think it best to continue on, and when we stop tomorrow night, I will bring you the story. I need to reflect on Captain Cook's first journey into this area when dispatched from England.

"Also, Bligh and Christian became more or less a combined story. One to explain Bligh being let down into the longboat and his journey, and at the same time, where Christian goes from there! I promise you a good story to bring some realization into those happenings back in the

1700s, Bligh's unbelievable long journey striking out to Jakarta and how he gets back to England! Also Fletcher Christian's journey in the opposite and how things ended up.

"Cook and Bligh both made journeys into the unknown, as well as the Melanesians who came here from who knows where? They settled and developed these islands. Fiji natives, for one, amaze me. From ancient explorers, charting their courses without instruments, relying on the sun, the moon, and the stars, and feeling the currents of the sea to chart their course.

"Instruments or tools of any kind developed their food, both plant and animal, to supplement their needs. An ancient people who have evolved from primitive to modern state-of-the-art country, so to speak, that has many islanders and countries depending on their knowledge as almost profound authority on education, technology, and medicine."

The thatched roof went silent as we spoke! "Yes," said Magnus. "And that is a story in itself! Well, James, we will be looking forward to the 'fate of the mutineers!'"

"That's a promise, and I might have to add a little Captain James Cook into the mix! Tomorrow, we head to Bligh Waters and beyond."

There wasn't a whole lot of sleep for us that night. Each mate tied up with his own thoughts. Early in the morning, a good breakfast compliments of the people from whom we borrowed the Chris-Craft. With a grin, Magnus cranked up his engines, and we were off. The two-Chrysler engine shifting that boat across the water, we were heading for Bligh Water.

When we were halfway across the designated area Bligh Water, Magnus coasted to a stop, shut off engines. We sat quietly and observed the water. Hawk asked, "Is this all of Bligh Water?"

I said, "No, it extends to Tonga."

Curt asked, "Was Bligh put off here?"

I said, "No, he was put off about forty miles south of Tonga."

Magnus spoke. "We will set here awhile as a tribute to William Bligh." It seemed like the proper thing to do. After some time, Magnus got up and pulled a pint of rum from under his dash. He popped the cap and threw the bottle toward the south island.

"There you go, mate. Mr. Bligh, your last ration of rum to you, old boy. You had a good run!" Then he looked at us all with a big grin and said, "I thought that was a fittin' tribute!"

I said, "I do, too, Magnus. Bligh would be proud!"

We started up again and moved through the Bligh Waters between the two major islands of Fiji. To the north on the course map, there was an island, very small, called Yadua Tabu. It was marked with a No Entry sign. I asked Magnus why that was so. He replied that he did not know. Since it was marked, he never ventured in. It could be a private island or maybe one that was sacred to the people.

We ventured on, and Magnus said we were going to the western out islands, off major island Viti Levu. He had some friends on the south point of this island chain, Waya, south off the Yasaw group. The other islands get quite busy with tourists.

This island, Magnus said, is more secluded, natural, and promises a nice accommodation in a thatched veranda with good food. They also have a torch-lighting ceremony like we experienced on the last stop. It was a beautiful place.

After we docked, Magnus led us in and, of course, the proprietor was another good friend of Magnus. They had a big greeting. Then Magnus turned and made the introductions to us. We were treated very well and settled into our quarters for the night.

Then Vanati, the proprietor, had our meal carried into the veranda. Yams, vegetables, and baked fish, sweets for dessert. Very delicious. We explored the little island, and as soon as it started to get dark, a bonfire was lighted outside our quarters, and a torch-lighting ceremony took place along the other dwellings there off the beach.

We sat and gazed into the fire, just enjoying the peace and quiet, and Hawk spoke up! "Okay, story time. Let's hear about the mutineers!"

"Okay, I will continue our story. But let me say, I have to go back to the point where Bligh is put off the *Bounty*. Everything gets really intertwined here, and we are seeing two different directions at once! Bligh's journey and Fletcher Christian's journey.

"I also need to give a little more detail on the journeys of each, all the why, when, and where. Even if I run the risk of repeating myself. It is a long story, so Magnus may have to book an extra night here!"

Magnus laughed. "No problem, mate."

Captain Mobley said, "I never get tired of stories of the sea, James. I know that you have researched this and have it all down in your log!" Curt and Hawk said nothing!

"Bligh and his ship, the *Bounty*, were dispatched to go to Fiji since breadfruit, a food staple, was discovered by the outside world. Since cotton sources had dried up because of war in the States. Because of war, wealthy plantation owners scrambled offshore. Some collaborated with Austrian plantation owners to acquire areas in the South Pacific islands to have slaves and crops. Food sources could get serious.

"Fiji had developed this breadfruit plant to be used as a food source for their diet. So to many, this was the answer to feed slaves that were prevalent in the South Pacific islands and also in the Caribbean islands.

"England dispatched Bligh to go to Fiji with botanist, scientist, plus crew to obtain breadfruit and also plants. Breadfruit was to be taken back to the Caribbean to feed slaves, since England was in this venture, too, because they needed the cotton! The long journey to Fiji went like this: leave England, travel the Atlantic to the Cape of Good Hope around South America, to the South Pacific. Long and tedious journey.

"Also King George wanted some plants in the botanical garden! So the admiralty used this to persuade the king to help finance these journeys! All went fairly well on this journey, except for the normal irritation that a crew gets on a long and tedious journey.

"On another trip, the *Bounty* and Bligh dispatched, left England, traveled the Atlantic to the top of South

America to round the cape. This ship was stopped because of severe storms. So blocked, they had to backtrack across the Atlantic to the cape around the bottom of Africa, sail through the Indian Ocean, then into the Pacific and up to Fiji.

"On this trip, the breadfruit harvest was still five months away! So you can imagine all the tension of this long journey on the crew and Bligh's nerves. The crew was disgruntled as well as Bligh! Captain Bligh ran a tight ship. He came up through the ranks with Captain Cook. Bligh used Cook's diet to feed his men to keep them healthy and made them dance regularly to keep them fit! You can imagine what that did to their morale, even though it was therapeutic!

"So five months delay gave the crew time to find girl-friends and other activities to their enjoyment. When the time came to leave, the crew were not too happy to return to cold, wet, dreary England. So some got their heads together, led by Fletcher Christian!

"Somewhere twenty to forty miles off the coast of Tonga, it came down! Bligh and twenty-six of his loyalists were put over in a twenty-three-foot ship's longboat. There was no more room for six more loyalists that had to stay aboard the *Bounty* with Christian. Bligh is given a watch, magnifying glass, and sextant, plus one week's ration of food for twenty-six men. One week!

"It was four thousand miles to Jakarta, which to Bligh was the shortest journey to safety and friendly Dutch hosts. The men were put on one ounce of bread and one ounce of water per day. Bligh enforced.

"They came across an island and stopped to investigate. As soon as one man stepped off the blow to secure the boat, natives attacked. As he is trying to push the boat back offshore, he is killed. One man down! Bligh continued on course, and along the way, some smaller islands appeared safe, and they went ashore to find food to supplement their diet.

"Bligh and crew had traveled around six hundred miles. A schooner traveling to Jakarta spotted them. They were picked up and taken on to Jakarta. There, the big East India shipping company gave passage to the group to proceed to England. Bligh had made a fantastic journey in history!

"When they neared England in the Pacific, they spotted an English Navy warship. Bligh was transferred to the navy ship and made it back to England. He reported the mutiny to the admiralty. They dispatched the HMS *Pandora* to proceed to the South Pacific and search for the mutineers.

"Now back to the Pacific. After Bligh is put down in the waters, Christian headed up the *Bounty* and sailed for Tahiti. Christian makes it to Tahiti with mutineers and six loyalists. After a stay on Tahiti, he decides to take the *Bounty* on to Pitcairn Island.

"Pitcairn Island, at this time, was an uncharted island. So to Christian, it is a safe haven. He rounds up the crew, and fourteen decide to stay in Tahiti. Six of the group are the loyalists who could not fit into the boat with Bligh.

"Christian also invites sixteen islanders on the *Bounty* for a tour. Once they are tricked on, he sets sail! The islanders are trapped. At Pitcairn Island, he burns the *Bounty* so no one can leave, and his pursuers will not spot the *Bounty*.

"Life goes on with Christian and the crew and sixteen islanders from Tahiti. Eventually some of the crew marry nine islanders. Now after marrying the women, the crew members are acting a bit superior to the island men. A fight resumes, and the islanders, in anger, rise up and kill the men! Hatred festers up within the women, and they rise up and kill the men!

"So unless I am confused, a recount. Fletcher Christian left Tahiti with eight mutineers, six Tahitian men, and eleven women. Sixteen crew members stayed in Tahiti, mutineers, plus the six loyalists. On the fifteenth day of January 1790, Fletcher Christian departs Tahiti for Pitcairn Island.

"During the same time, Bligh is on his long siege to safety. On his return to England, he reports the mutiny. The admiralty dispatches the HMS *Pandora* to the South Pacific to hunt down the mutineers. Of course, the journey takes the long route around to the South Pacific from England in the north Atlantic.

"The *Pandora*, on its search, finally arrives in Tahiti. There are fourteen survivors left. The *Pandora* gathers them up, disregarding the loyalists, takes them all prisoner. They failed to find Fletcher Christian, so they begin their journey back to England. Some of the prisoners were cuffed, and some were put in cages on deck!

"As the *Pandora* proceeded west with the intent to return to England by the Indian Ocean and around the horn of Africa, it ran into the Great Barrier Reef off northern Australia, and the *Pandora* went down! Many died, crewmen and prisoners alike! What crew and prisoners that survived were taken to Jakarta. The Dutch Shipping Company there provided passage back to England for all these poor survivors from mutiny and shipwreck that came straggling in.

"The crown of England was billed for all this. When the group returned to England, survivors off the *Bounty* were put on trial. Four were requited, three were pardoned, and three were hanged. The free out of the trial were allowed to resume their position in the navy.

"So they were never able to find Fletcher Christian until 1808, when an American ship docked at Pitcairn Island, the first ship to dock at the island since the *Bounty*. Fletcher had died in 1793 at the age of twenty-eight! So his life was short-lived!

"There was only one survivor left from the *Bounty*, plus a whole group of descendants of mixed people from Fletcher and the crew.

"Now after that, as Bligh continued his career, he once again sailed with his mate, Captain Cook. This was Cook's last journey, and Bligh was his headmaster. They were dispatched to go to the north coast of Siberia, enter the Bering Sea to assist with an exploration group searching for the Northwest Passage.

"Twice into the Bering Sea, they were turned back by the ice, so that journey was futile! This is when Cook and Bligh touched the southern tip of Alaska. Tried to help a group there, but no success. So returning south, Captain

Cook made his second visit to Hawaii, where he met his death in a battle with the Polynesians.

"I can't confirm how his body was handled, but I do know that he was buried at sea. I would presume that Master Bligh, now Captain Bligh of the *Endeavor*, second-in-command, officiated the burial rites!

"So, gentlemen, that is all I can offer you. There is so much history intermixed with the lives of these two great men that it is hard to relate. I only wish I knew and could write that story because I know that it would be the greatest book or novel that a man could write!" As I looked around at the group quietly sitting in silence, Magnus had tears in his eyes!

"Sorry, mate," he said. "But they were my two greatest heroes in my lifetime!"

Captain Mobley was next. "Fine go, James. If you could get all that down in a log, mate, it will be great!"

Curt and Hawk looked at me astonished! Hawk finally spoke up. "Wow, James. I don't believe I could tell all that story on a plane trip!"

Curt addressed Hawk. "Tell it at a piece of a time, dummy! Then folks would have to take another flight to get the rest of the story!" We all laughed. It was a good night.

In the morning, we got underway again. Magnus took us down slowly through the rest of the chain of islands for a look-see. As we rounded the bottom of Viti Levu, he asked, "Do you boys want to see the little group of islands on the eastside of Viti Levu? Mostly tourist-improved?"

Curt spoke up, "No thanks, Magnus. We are so grateful for this time together, but we must get back. Hawk and I have tourist flights scheduled in Samoa."

So Magnus hits the throttle, and we had a good run seeing the islands on the way, back to our point of departure at the shopping center dock. We escorted Magnus to the dockside when we stopped. We thanked him for a wonderful time and journey.

Hawk said, "No need to get back on your boat, Uncle Magnus! Just take the free bus back to the Radisson! I want you to promise me you won't swim out to your boat anymore! I want to keep you around now that we have gotten together!"

"I promise," Magnus said with a chuckle. "My clients will have to meet me here! Now you get back and see me once in a while."

Hawk said, "I will, Uncle Magnus!" And they embraced. We shook hands all around and gave our "Thank yous." Magnus was climbing back into his boat, and we were heading for the plane.

We taxied out into the harbor, hit the throttle, and were airborne into time, heading for Sydney! I was quiet in the flight. Captain Mobley asked, "What's on your mind, mate?"

I answered, "Captain, that last cruise we took! All the cruises we were on together was almost a repeat of all the places Captain Cook ventured to. Maybe not in the same way, but a lot of the places he ventured to, so have we! I'm just glad that our last cruise didn't end in Hawaii! That was the last cruise Captain Cook was ever to make!"

Captain Mobley thought for a moment and replied, "That's right, mate. I'm glad too! I really didn't plan the cruises by Captain Cook. It was just places I wanted to see, not to track him! But I see what you mean, mate!" He paused. "But I don't think it will be an end to our time together, do you?"

I replied, "Well, I hope not, Captain. If we can just keep going!"

Sydney was on the horizon! We would fly back into the harbor, and Captain Mobley and I would depart, and Curt and Hawk would be heading for Samoa!

The long farewell

Near the end of our trip, Captain Mobley had confided in me that back to Sydney, there will be no welcome home party. With the crew gone and ladies with them, there wasn't a need this time. I agreed. Curt and Hawk had tourist commitments back in Samoa, and Captain had things needing addressed on the station that he did not want Sheila and Dick to handle by themselves. I wanted to move on out also. The party was over. None of us leaving in a bad way but in a contented way.

With the Sydney Harbour in sight now, it was a glorious sight. Sunny day, calm water, and the plane easing down gentle-like for a smooth landing. We touched down, Hawk throttled back, and we were taxiing for the pier. We all climbed out, let the engine running slow. Tied a steady line!

We had our little chat, and then Hawk turned to me. "James, it has been a pleasure. Perhaps some time we will get together again? Maybe a trip to Canada to see your friend Eagle Feather and spend a few days at camp? I can fly in without fear, for thanks to Curt, I am now an American citizen. We could just fly into Mountain Ash Lake. I'll land like old times, taxi to the pier!"

I asked, "How will you contact Eagle Feather in that vast north woods?"

He chuckled. "Indians have their way of communication!" We then shook hands all around, pats on the back and such. When Hawk released my hand, he raised my elbow up and his also, lay together and clasped hands! I knew what that meant. I was honored!

We held in that position for a moment, then he said, "James, we are blood brothers now. I always will remember you!"

I looked into his eyes. "Hawk, I am proud to be your brother, and I will never forget you! Our paths must cross again!"

With that and handshakes all around again, Curt and Hawk untied and boarded the plane. Captain and I watched as that beautiful teal blue and white aircraft taxied into the bay. Hawk pushed the throttle forward, and they smoothly skipped across the water and were airborne and quickly out of sight!

Captain said, "Well, James, we are the last of the Mohicans!"

"I guess I will get busy and call for a taxi. Need to get to the airport and book in, Captain!"

"No need, mate. I already called ahead for two. Mine will be here directly, and Leilani is coming for you! I hope you don't mind that I imposed? She has an off day, and the airline owes her a free trip. So, mate, you have a companion to LA!"

His cab was pulling in, and he said, "This is it, mate." He shook my hand and gave me a big bear hug! I returned it. As he was getting in the cab, he paused. With misty eyes, he stared at me for a long moment. "The best to you, mate! It has been a good go, and we must stay in touch!"

"We will," I said. The taxi pulled away, and I was on the dock alone, trying to figure what was coming down! Another taxi pulled up, and Leilani jumped out, ran to me, and flung her arms around me with a big kiss! I didn't know what to say, just stunned.

"Come on. We are late." The taxi whisked us to the airport. We obtained our boarding passes and entered the plane. I was still in awe!

On the plane, Leilani said to me, "Captain Mobley purchased your tickets. Mine is a free flight that the airlines owe me. Two seats in first class, just like you always preferred. This time, I will occupy the second seat if you don't mind." And she giggled.

"I don't mind, Lei. I will have you all flight instead of your duty breaks on our other flights."

"What?" she exclaimed! "James, you called me Lei!"

"I'm sorry, Leilani. I guess I was a little out of place!"

"No, no! I like you calling me 'Lei.' It makes me feel that we are together, like a couple!"

We settled in, first class, and all to ourselves! No other seats taken. Our flight attendant was named Rachel, and she was a workmate of Lei's. We received first class treatment, above and beyond the normal. Rachel brought us blankets, and Lei and I settled down in the double seats. We cuddled down close! And waited for last call before the takeoff. It felt so good after being alone for so long by myself!

We were off! Climbing high and starting through the time zones. Darkness fell, and so did we, fast asleep. As in previous flights, Leilani sat with me at night call when off duty. She always fell asleep on my shoulder, and I always felt so warm and alive! Nothing serious ever occurred between us.

As we proceeded through the darkness, like other flights, I was stirred by this little voice from paradise, which could talk to me a short time. Earth time, that is, because paradise is not timebound!

As usual, Anita came on again. I stirred and said, "Is that you, Skipper?"

"Yes, Jamie, it is. Looking in on you, I see your companion is with you again." I started to speak to explain. "Shush, honey. I just have a small space here, and I want to tell you a couple of things before I am again pulled away! Baby, you have been alone for five long years. It is time to love and forget grief. When your time is up, you will come to me, I know that. You need to know I love you and always will. But for now, my love, you must follow your heart!"

Then like always, it faded away. It left me quite shaken. Follow your heart? So I lay quietly and shaken, stayed still so I would not disturb Leilani sleeping peacefully at my side.

Dawn broke, and Rachel arrived with warm cloths and a nice breakfast. She said we had time because arrival at LA would be another hour. I started to feel really sad and depressed. What was this goodbye going to bring? I never did like goodbyes!

On schedule, we touched down, then my heart dropped. To the terminal we went, and the exit tunnel was sent to the plane. The passengers were departing!

I looked at Lei and said, "I am so sorry, Lei, but this is it!"

Lei looked at me, and a tear started to run down her cheek! With misty eyes, I took my thumb and brushed it away. I pulled her close in my arms. I pulled her close and kissed her softly on the lips.

"Don't leave me, James! I love you! Stay with me and come to Samoa!"

"Oh, baby, I love you so much, but I can't do that!"

"James, don't leave me. I love you! Stay with me and come to Samoa!"

I was stricken. My mind was whirring. I was thinking responsibility, commitment, promises. All this whirring around in my mind!

Again, "I love you, James. Do you know that?"

I said nothing.

"I want you, James. I love you, and I need you. I will always take care of you!"

We paused, and Leilani released me and stepped back. Her eyes pleading, she softly spoke. "Is it what you said to

Captain Mobley? That we were in two different worlds? One was worlds apart, and the other was ages apart! James, my love does not measure distance apart, nor does it recognize age. What it measures is two hearts coming together and falling in love."

Leilani came into me again, put her arms around me, and I kissed her passionately! Her eyes, her cheek, her lips. Then she said, "I love you so much, *Jamie*!"

That startled me, and I raised her chin. "You have been listening?"

She smiled a little smile and said to me, "Yes, Jamie. I have been listening since the very first flight. What was said this time was different. I think your wife in heaven looked down on you and picked me to look after you! What did she say to you, Jamie? She said you must follow your heart. I love you, and I said love sees no bounds. I want you, and I will always love you and take care of you! Come with me to Samoa!"

Rachel was standing by, and we didn't care. Just doing her job! "Mr. James, are you going to depart?" She went and was closing the passenger hatch. The departure ramp had been retracted. She came back. "Sorry, Mr. James. Captain says last call. You will have to depart now."

I looked at Rachel, then at Leilani. "Give me one moment." I took Lei in my arms and kissed her with passion, then I turned to Rachel. "I'm not getting off the plane! Tell your captain to proceed!"

Rachel keyed her mic and spoke! "All clear, Captain. Mr. James says he is not getting off the plane! He is not leaving! He says for you to give it a good go! Two passengers in first class are leaving with you, and the destination is Samoa!" Rachel laughed, and Leilani jumped into my arms, found my lips, and gave me a most passionate kiss.

We heard the pilot answer back to Rachel, "I roger that call, Rachel" And then he shouted, "Checkmate!" And we started rolling down the runway! Rachel clipped into a seat and buckled up.

She looked at me and said, "You two better take your seat and buckle up! We will be in flight soon!"

I looked at Rachel with a grin. "Rachel, we are already in flight!" Leilani was holding me so tight, like I could never get away! We were Samoa-bound!

Author's Comments

Imagination is a wonderful thing. It allows you to travel the seas with an imaginary captain and friend, to travel to exotic places in the mind. Sometimes it becomes real, especially if you put your own real travels into the mix.

My story mate, Linn Hartman, in his younger days, spent an actual cruise on the HMS *Endeavor* (replica), Captain James Cook's ship. The replica of the *Endeavor* has traveled to many ports, once berthed in Australia.

The HMS *Bounty* was lost. Fletcher Christian burned it at Pitcairn Island in the South Pacific. Captain William Booth was set with twenty-six loyalists but made the journey to Jakarta (Dutch), losing only one man.

Captain Bligh, after rescue, was dispatched with Captain James Cook on the Aleutian Island Bering Sea expedition to search for the Northwest Passage. On return, Hawaii was Cook's second journey there. In a battle with Polynesians, he was killed! He was buried at sea. No doubt his friend and mate, William Bligh, in charge of ceremony. Bligh, in later years, was promoted to admiral in the English Navy.

The HMS *Pandora* was dispatched from England to search for the mutiny survivors and captured fourteen at Tahiti. Returning to England, they ran aground on the

Great Barrier Reef off northern Australia. Most all were lost. Australia has raised the HMS *Pandora* from its watery grave in the reef and has put it on display.

The history facts on these two sea heroes are an exciting read. I only wish I had time to write a complete novel on such!

Thank you to my readers.

About the Author

James left the east at the age of seventeen to join the navy and serve his country. He says, "I am now eighty-seven years old, and I live on this farm with my dog, Cocoa. I am about to bring you a story from the figment of my imagination. It is a fictional story based on facts about my travels around the world during my time with the US Navy and trips with my late wife, Anita."

With the support and encouragement from Anita, he has put pen to paper to share the wild adventures of his heart and mind.

Also by James Gardner:

Novelettes:
- *The Quest for Quanah*
- *Return of the White Wolf*
- *Odyssey Down Under*
- *Odyssey Down Under Parts II and III*

Short stories:
- "A Winter's Tale"
- "Suzeane and James"